T0285026

THE
SEMPER FI

by David Musick

The door goes 'click' and the curtain rises. It's showtime, under the midnight sun of hallway lights in haunted towns. I listen as my shoes go 'clump'. I follow the sound hypnotically, willingly. It's all I got. It's all a dog has got.

Except I am not moving. The clumping sound I hear is from the ten thousand and one transits I have made of the hallway, phantom steps I can feel in my sleep. For I have stood since the door went silent, stuck to the jamb like a short-sighted spider crushed by the door of his tomb.

My guts you see have spilled onto the carpet, what guts I had. The guts that fired into the tree line, 'thook' 'thook' 'thook', in that war long ago, 600 yards, not even seeing the dead, dead before the rattle of the gun had reached them; the guts that killed an old man in Chicago, sure, the man who killed my buddy Charlie, pure revenge, fired by liquor. I had those kinds of guts. The yellow kind.

I didn't have the murdering kind, that was all, the cold-blooded kind; I didn't have guts at all it seems. Not for Evans, whose hand was surely on the trigger that killed Charlie; not for the Lover Boy, whose perversion muddied the beautiful pond that God had granted us.

"Keep God out of this, Maddock."

Let them wrestle it out, then…it will be my little peep show, everything tidy in my little world. Put Charlie to rest, lock the closet, kick the toys under the bed, head to Florida and Marie, the one good thing. Let them tear it all asunder, then finish the plan, step 6 or 7, I forget, the drive southeast to the coast, start the new life.

So off down the hallway I shuffle, the hall to the stairwell, down one last time, closer to hell. Down the hallway, down the stairs, down.

I sit in the car in the basement garage, and I think about it all again. This plan was wry already, little chance for success; shoot the Lover Boy, shoot Evans, imprint the gun and drop the gun to the floor. Can I really make it out the back, four stories down, into the car, off to the east and on down to the coast? Not likely.

I suppose I had the guts, maybe. But why take the chance? Let Evans shoot the bastard, let the cops make their play, let the devil dance, I don't owe nobody nothing.

There is always a plan, there always is. And as sure as sunrise this plan rose up before me. And this new one I hatched, this frame and getaway plan, fresh-baked when the apartment door went 'click', well, my hands will be clean. Clean hands and a dirty mind. The peep and run plan we shall call it...

It was late now as I cranked the engine over and put her in gear. I headed up to street-level and out. I always loved the dark...

MADDOCK

I showered in the trucker's lounge at Rip's, the free water two bucks a towel shower that's hotter than sin in Sin City. I was shook all right, a large nerve making my thigh jump and it was all I could do to hold onto the soap - but the hot water helped and the stream of heat kept me from thinking.

I toweled off in a hurry, shaved less hurried and crawled into a pair of jeans and blue cotton work shirt. I slipped on boots and tucked my shades into the shirt pocket and buttoned it down. I left a ball cap on the dash of the car in case I made sunrise. I wadded up the running suit and ditched it inside a backpack I brought my change of clothes in. I figured to burn it all later on. The pack over my shoulder, I grabbed the shaving kit by the loop and headed outdoors, stepping into the far moment.

It was dark outside and warm, 70 degrees maybe and dry as Aunt Matilda. No clouds, the sky buck naked and wide open as anything. Three a.m. and a million stars and a nice night to linger but I had a ways to go and no end to that. What I'd done and what the stars had seen I didn't even want to look up. Just keep on rambling. So I made a beeline for the car and climbed on board and turned the engine over and backed around and out. I was on the freeway again in ten seconds flat.

The road out was sparse and quick, faster than a meadowlark but not fast enough. I got it to seventy on a smooth rise and eased it back a notch and slowly began to draw breath once again – enough to keep the lights on anyway. I was tight for sure and nowhere near ready for people. Not much for company. That first sixty miles had gone by in the tick of a clock and the bright lights and clatter of cups and the trucks idling and all the eighteen-wheel loafers standing around, counting their miles. No thanks buddy, I'd rather keep moving. Take it the short way across. No friends, no eyeballs picking my pocket.

So back on the road and out, to where there was nothing but nothing and no one around, only the oncoming headlights like souls going home and not many of those at that hour. No edge, no horizon either, just a smooth black slate and broken white line racing away down the middle. One or two points of light here and there and a faded old moon fixing to rise now and dangle somewhere above it all. Laughing most likely. A laughing moon and wind too, the thin kind with fingers at the windows whispering. It was that kind of night. And around it all the engine was just plain sorrowful with all the moaning and groaning.

If I wasn't before I was plenty shook now, the adrenaline wearing off fast and no recourse but to hold tight as the life story wheeled by, this evening's load and every load back to the beginning and all that went between. That whole big laugh parade. Take a swig of your story, amigo, and follow it down the way you always drank it - one case at a time. Chase it like you need a life, that old joker.

"Only don't waste your breath, Maddock. You never buy nothing."

So I fiddled with the backpack where it lay on the floorboard, trying to finish zipping it or not and hold the road too and gave up on that, back to counting the dashes, watching them play at making a line. The way I played at making a life. And nobody standing on the roadside waving. Not a soul. No 'Hey Mack, need some company?' Not in that dark. Lucky, too. You ever been alone you'll know what I mean. Plenty black and plenty of it. And nothing, not anything holding back the night. Just you on your end and everything there ever was on the other and the engine droning still, bawling away inside my head. 'I am, I am' it glowered, my heart banging along in time.

"Roy Rogers and his Drunken Clock," I leered. A coward's bluff and didn't I know it. I hadn't yet given up on going yellow, you see.

So I clicked the radio and twisted the dial, night music for my little nest. To slow things down, a calmative for the mind. A relief once removed, like an echo, like a hollow friend. I gave a glance to the dark flowing by, at a familiar face trotting alongside, yellow and blue from the dash lights and looking a lot like me; dried out was all and more or less dead. I shivered with a laugh while it wavered and smiled…

…and tuned a country station out of Kansas while fiddling with the cruise control and wrestling with a thermos of hot coffee. One second later I ditch the thermos and grab a real one out of the duffel on the back seat. I needed my wits. Coffee's grand but liquor trumps and I snagged the goods with my free hand dangling over. Dragging the bottle out of the sack, the 12-gauge clanked, a

Wingmaster, laying there like a hard-on and I tried to remember why but gave up on that. No room in the trunk on account of the big guest list. That must have been it.

Flash-primed and jaunty as a cork, I took a long, determined pull on the jug, my left eye dialed in on the centerline. Like following a thread on plush black carpet. Or plummeting down in the night. What all my training was for, that crack of intuition, the moment of truth. Ready, aim, fire! cries the gumshoe…

I came up for air and drained another, a real haymaker to smooth things out. I lit a smoke and clucked like a hen.

'Why look back?' the mind begged to wonder. To remember…what? Throwing up smoke was all, the little mind and its little mind games.

I sneaked a drag on the cigarette and waited for some sort of answer. All the while impatient eyes danced about the cabin, peeped from the rearview, tired old friends dropped by for a visit. Sideways eyes lit up and glowing and giddy with fear. Taunting eyes that dared me peer within. As embers of cigarette and dash light haze cast a harlequin mask of my face on the windshield. A mouth laughed, my mouth, its dim shadow etched on a looking glass in Neverland.

"File it under tough luck," I growled and glanced away quick - but not quick enough. My reflection was back, wavering outside the car again, floating, jeering, galloping along in the night.

"Well, well," I said, jerked my eyes away good and firm and grinned myself a big one. So, it was going to be that sort of show.

"Enjoy the ride," I implored and placed a modest bet on the future, an ounce and a half and ran it down with aplomb. Plunging headlong into the well now, ankles wriggling, the grip beginning to unwind.

"Steady as she goes," piped the captain and I tightened my grasp, letting the music pull me out slow and easy, like a quick one in the alley.

The song blowing from the radio was "Wichita Lineman," Glen singing his ballad real warm and tender, the broadcast flowing out from the title city itself, five hundred miles to the southeast now, over that stretch of ground known once, in the bygones, as the Cherokee Strip. Forgotten ground, though sacred to the tribes I figured, near the end at least, and wide as an ocean. Wide enough for a last stand…until smaller and smaller and finally gone. The way a drop of water disappears. The way a heart goes dry.

Dead too the language I figured, Wichita, up in smoke. I'd be passing it wide in an hour or so, bearing south, a couple hundred miles west of it, about the time I crossed Sand Creek, that other slaughter with its unsettled spirits and the ground around it everywhere drenched with them. Ground better crossed at daybreak I guess, which accounted for my willies, the hairs waving on my neck to the music in time. You'd have to be dead to not feel the spirits and I felt them and no lie.

But the car kept rolling and the song kept lifting me slow, the memories flowing back slower still, of drive-in theaters and beer drinkin' with the boys and all those back roads at night and the tall tales that never were. Not a flood of memory, but heavy, like raising the dead. All that bluffing a long time gone and cold like it never was. Still, something comforting about the melody, the remembrance of it. Something good to hold onto if you could just find the handle. Memories, you'll find, the fatal kind, don't range so far.

I reached for the dashboard lighter and lit another smoke and this time I puffed in a measured way, studying the rearview in the glow of ember. Real suave, checking my eyes very carefully, trying to get a lead on where things stood, where things were heading. Taking a gander inside but standing not so very close to the edge. Feeling the need to agree on something, as if everything hinged on it. Pushing to arrive at a conclusion, but only so hard. Letting the car drive itself and the miles roll by and letting my mind have some rope - but holding it close. I might have a use for it someday, my little mind.

Everything had gone smooth, nothing went haywire with the plan. Like when the house burns so hot there's nothing left to bag. From my side everything went smooth. Nothing to sweep up, no rag to prod with a stick. Nice powdery ash, help yourself. No sense of the box canyon, the tight squeeze either. This didn't have the feel of those. Clean, if I had to put a word to it. No mess, the whole plan was done clean. Up to step six that is…five of the first half dozen steps anyway, the hard ones, spit-shined like soldiers all in a row. Oh, I might have dropped a stitch somewhere in step 6, like not shooting Lover Boy and Evans myself, but hey, I winged the guy that was waiting to blow my brains out and knocked the other one down it appeared, permanent perhaps, or so it seemed. I surely racked up points on that score. Which didn't widen the ledge I was toeing or steady my balance. I was still dangling. Nerves was all…I guess I was counting my nerves and no surprise there.

A couple hours, a hundred miles since I kicked off step number six. Lucky six, last in the plan. The step you write home about, before the rush to a new reality. It was my plan all right, all mine, and it had worked in my head just fine. Trouble was, nobody told me deuces were wild. Oh tut.

So, despite a somewhat slick outcome, what with all the moving parts, a cool weak flame still flickered inside. It licked at my guts and left me hanging by a thought.

"Keep it simple," I reminded myself. "And don't forget the ammo," I said and tugged at my collar. It was getting awful crowded inside.

"Might as well get used to it, to sleeping with one eye open," I pouted.

"You'll get used to it," I said as the words tumbled from my mouth, ran about the cabin like little blind mice. But the words would not connect. I was too far-gone thinking.

I drove that way another sixty miles, shook up, sweating some and only pulled over the once, into a rest area.

Circled by a tall coven of pines, amidst a prairie grassland running from one end of a dark night world to the other, outside the human circle and alone beneath an accusatory sky, I stepped from the car. It was a strange notion, and I knew it was strange, but I needed to put it to rest. Eerie almost, this feeling I had of a blood trail following the car. A thin, clotted black line tracking its way back to the horizon. I was that whacked out. I even began but managed to stop myself before opening the car's trunk in that dark. Like staring into your own casket and didn't I know it.

"It's you and me now, Maddock, like it always was."

Spoken but not heard. Just cold, quaking ground underfoot and no help nowhere. I shuddered in the heat.

Stumbling in such a fearful darkness, tired and strung out as a hung jury, I answered the wake-up call - a sharp, nasty jolt it was, that struck deep and finished me off with a shiver. It was the one about human flesh.

I made it back to the driver's side door and fell in. Maybe I crawled, I wouldn't know, I was alone and no one to tell me.

"Nerves," I muttered but who was listening. Even the wind had gone silent now. Just a shallow, ragged cough as the engine fired and turned over, the gravel hissed and then I was gone.

Nothing remained but the crackling stars.

AT THE CORRAL

Down the bend that runs from Limon to Lamar, the eighty miles or so that begins the turn south, all the way down I was glancing over my shoulder. The question which raised itself more than once, "what if?" was followed by a pause so long and deep and cold that I was reminded of the ocean. A vast, empty space and no hurry to color it in either. My hole card was emptiness. Let fate pass me over and never ante up, make the bet. Just hold it for the last hand. Hold it for luck. I figured I was due.

So I managed a meditation to open mind and heart, clear a path to that peace which resides with emptiness. A rare find, emptiness. I could use it to begin again. It was what I had left. Find something to grow inside it. That or let the other thing gnaw its fill. Gorge until nothing. The other side of empty. Either way a nail-biter, so maybe close your eyes and toss a coin, skip the hard part. Picking sides would only get me to thinking again. And nothing more dangerous than a mind on the loose.

And so I drifted back to those early days. A whole lifetime ago it now seemed. I'd left a nice arrangement in the city, falling away over the shoulder now, a few hundred miles back and falling away fast. Call it a garden. The city version of one and the crop it grew was money. You watered it and did the grubbing and weeding and over time, enough long hours, you made out. The whole business founded on the predictability of human nature. It was the straightest, easiest, most reliable source of cash one could imagine. People being less wary than rats and nearly as vulgar. Most of the time they didn't eat their babies, but that was about where the line was drawn.

You made a job of it, but nothing could shake the facts. You were still a farmer. You hung out a sign and sat by the phone. Someone was going to gouge or bust or cheat your client. He or she would readily fork over a wad of twenties that you might stand in the doorway and prevent them the pain. Palm to palm and strictly legit.

That or someone's pubic zone was on fire and needed an itch and your client was flaming out and throwing money at the pyre. You were a laborer in the house of deceit, and you sold your sweat and there were plenty of takers. Lines of them, all dying to live. Nervous piles of flesh. And they knocked down the door, imploring you to fix it, keep it good, make their five-minute lives whole again. They were the whores and you ran the house. Somehow, some nights, it made you better than them. It was easier that way.

There were the decent people also, who had strayed from the path or had been conned or just unlucky and those you helped too, only by now you were dirty and they made you remember and that was uncomfortable. So you sent them a bill and added ten percent for giving you a pain. Maybe you did a free one, a white-hat special occasionally, but somehow I just don't remember.

It often got rough but you knew that and expected that and were ready for that when it happened. If you weren't, you were out of the game. The only rule and simple, really. No tears, no shoulder to cry on. And a regular freak show on the dark days. More than likely a laugh on the others, if you were disposed that way, if you liked the human pratfall.

At night you earned your liquor hard. Mornings brought the cigarettes and coffee, the day all shiny and ready to spar. Simple. Maybe too simple. In a predictable sort of way you wanted, you *felt* you had a whippin' coming. Meddler's guilt I called it. All the dicks I knew were head cases.

If you didn't mind slumming with the people, getting dirty yourself, you cashed in. It was a garden all right, just not the one in Eden. None of those you dealt with had a foot in that one, not for long.

So they queued up at your door, a line that wrapped clear round the block. If you ever wonder why, just ask one of the smart guys. There are still plenty of those lounging about, the bright boys with all the answers. Boatloads of bright boys. I know, I was one of them a short while back, used to be until I fell from grace. Slipped. Sailing along real smooth until the day I believed my own lines. Fatal, the moment you see the world through your own filter. The big sin in my business and appalled I didn't see it coming.

So there you lay in a pile with all the other little guys. The bright boys. And when you're out, brother, you're tossed for good and there's no easy way back. Least not for me. To the garden I mean. After a time, you forget the place ever existed. And amen to that.

Or you fall from the stool your mug stuck to the floor. Maybe you grab a rung and dust yourself off or somebody holds out a hand.

Whatever. The story doesn't matter, neither the leg up nor the lay down. Tell it on your own time mister, the big story, but keep on moving. The way out is that-a-way and the door is closing...

.   .   .   .   .

Arriving Lamar, I parked and sat at idle in front of The Corral, the local cattlemen's steakhouse. Only for a moment's stretch and to finish a smoke and suck a little more of the cider.

The restaurant was done up in farmer brown, no nonsense, with a wooden rail and porch and the sign in white letters. The front door looked like a little corral with a couple bales stacked to one side and a rusty wagon wheel and a wooden barrel and lantern on top. The frontier look. And why not, we were in the middle of nowhere.

Leaning next to the place, its entrance off the far end, was an all-nighter, a familiar looking shed, dead ringer for a thousand other string town bars that crowded the mainline. One darked-out window and the front door wide open and a beer sign glowing like a pot of gold above the entrance. A lowball drink and dance emporium, a one-time chicken coop the town had grown around, the birds long flushed and a hose taken to it, with a keg and tables and unmatched chairs and sawdust thrown about. Made no mind to the new birds, the customers with their beer guts, talking to the calendar girls on the walls and cigarette smoke twirling to high heaven above the pool table. Music and smoke pouring out of the hole and a lot of coming and going for 5 a.m. A couple of cowboys with hats but no saddles and a couple cowgirls looking to bust 'em. A drunk or two and what looked like the mayor come to buy votes. Made you want to settle down, join the council. Except for the jukebox and breaking glass and shouts above the already loud rabble, it was real peaceful. A sedate, wild west tableau, and damn civilized at that.

I laughed if you could call it that and finished my smoke and coaxed another belt for the road. Then I sat up and stretched and got organized and ready to ride.

Back a mile the feedlot was smoldering, so I ran up the window as a trooper drove through the lot, making his rounds. He did a wide circle and cruised the front of the nightclub, one row over from where I was throwing my party. He stared in as he rolled past the gaping doorway - making sure all the bad eggs were accounted for. Then he wheeled around and headed back onto the main road. A black and white, so maybe county law.

"Money's in the trunk," I snickered and stubbed my cigarette and corked the flask. I was tickled now, full of grins when I put the car in gear and took a right from the lot heading south, traveling the same direction and trailing the cop, pulling in behind. We made a little caravan until a block before the city limits when he turned into the Country Cupboard, a clean-looking cafe with fresh paint and paved parking and the entry well lit. A nice place, a toothpicks by the register, mints at the door type of place with red and white checkered tablecloths and shiny flatware and milk-fed, husky girls peddling coffee in tennies and starched uniforms. And second income moms in sup-hose, glad to be out of the barn.

Joe Cop stopped for grits, with an eye to the new talent back from tech school, all growed up and working the counter. But I kept going, floored the mother.

"The biggest collar of his life a car length back and he settles for the Early Bird special," I laughed, kind of half-hearted, until I almost cried.

THE SET-UP

After that, nothing but a thin line on the map, ninety miles and quick unless you pull over to floss or jawbone with the farmer philosophers that hang around the gas pumps on the mainline, those highway oases with their licorice whips and gewgaws and mousetraps under the counter. Hanging around like ant lions and hungry for travelers. Explaining what they're doing in the middle of nowhere and a little guilty at that. Or just rocking on their heels, staring out at the fields. Standing guard on bumpkin America, the hinterlands. With their overalls and coin purses and mail order shoes.

Back in town they're the guys that'll work for food but seldom do and it's not hard to find a soft spot under each of them. Dashed on the rocks and at least four degrees smarter than I, which evoked a horse laugh that shook me out of my drift. I opened wide and gargled a drink as big as the great outdoors, big as Old Faithful, pressing my lips to hold it. I followed that with a lazy half-turn to the east, gazing into the faint, peach-colored haze rising slowly, like the Saturday morning curtain at the Bijou. Cast a long look east before I went over the set-up, such as it was.

The set-up went bang, clump, bang, bang, bang, drive to Amarillo. Fairly balanced even with the clump, which was me getting pounded and left like a meatball in a pool of red sauce.

Balanced and free and easy. No sweat unless you had a thing about homicide or cages or sleeping with tattooed roommates. Or got pinned beneath all the stiffs tumbling from the closet, a slumber party of stiffs. Balanced in the way choices never are, like loaded dice or the trapdoor out of town. That kind of whore.

Keyed-up and unable to restrain myself, I cover my eyes and pick door number three, the one with the dinette, and that makes me thirsty. I fish around the back seat for my bottle, bumping about in the dark. Warm and cozy I find it, room temperature for baby and four hours worth of formula. Enough to get me there in style, to the Motel El Rayo, round and round the circular drive. Turn in, flop out and roll onto the welcome mat. Home the pie-eyed PI. Close enough to smell the biscuits.

Still, a gray highway in that first light of day, first light of creation. No red carpet on this trip, the way I'd always planned. No victory lap for a job well done. Yet free, no rope on my neck, not any time soon. A little damp maybe, beneath the collar. But free, that most faithless of lovers.

Curious, I watch my hand as it slides beneath the seat, feel it touch the butt of the nine-millimeter I carry to make change. I bring it up slow and stare hard and long at the road. Both of us empty, the road and I. Flat and gray and running in tandem, pacing ourselves, not a word between us. The gun is something else again, holds seven and speaks volumes. Whispers to me, sells me all the old lies about death do us part. All the old lies I hung my life on. We listened well my ear and I, liked our odds plenty. Real solid and why not. At seventy-five mph and blowing 20 on the rum-dumb scale, with all them buckets of guns and booze and gas, we liked them just fine.

So hallelujah, I say! A lightning start to day number two, the world happily unhinged and me the grand marshal. Strike up the band as the spook parade marches past, with a clack of bones and tottering skull, and suddenly I smell the burning flesh and retch. There, in a puddle on the floorboard, I spy my merit badge. A bloody hairball, number five of nine, and me the lucky one. I run my sleeve over my mouth, still holding the gun and wait. For the earth to open and swallow the dead? Better the ocean swallow the earth...and pronto.

"You might want to lay off the stuff, Maddock," I says. But when the boat stops rocking, I put away the piece and have another belt. I been there before.

BACK WITH THE PLAN

Yeah, one of those guys. One of the thinkers. It brought me far my little gray friend, my very own ball of nerves. All the way from there to now. 'Listen,' it says. 'I'll tell you about it...spill a little...'

I got a late model sedan, loaded with booty. I got bank accounts and property and a suitcase full of cash. I got guns and bullets and plenty to shoot at. I got clothes for a week and three thousand miles of ground to cover. I ain't on nobody's call list and nobody blows their whistle at me…want more?

Got a girl? Check. A kind of one, a dream girl, the best kind of one. Got a plan? Check, you could call it so. And a past? No, not any longer. I sold that one. You got faith? Never did, forget why. Got the shakes? Yeah, but like an old friend, not so bad. You got a theme song? Sure, *Strangers In The Night*. No, make that *Stranger In Paradise*. Any booze? You got booze, don't you? Yeah, but not enough, there never was enough. Any friends? How about one down, two to go. Any hope? No hope. Truth? Yeah, plenty truth and a mouthful of lies…

I pull off the highway, follow the frontage road for a mile until I reach a county road and turn west, the sun at my back. I need to pull over, have it out. The body's okay but the mind is finished, tired of being preyed upon. I turn onto a dirt road, private property, no house in sight and cut the engine, roll to a stop. It's just me now, at the end of the line. All those long years ago have brought me here. All those glad hands. I light a cigarette and climb from the car, lean my arms on the roof and smoke. Nothing else makes sense and I draw on it greedily, I got nothing but time…

It doesn't have to end here. What I see is a choice. Drag it along, all the way to judgment day or cut the cord, shove it into the bag with all the other dead kittens. Tie off the sack and toss it into the river. Bury it deep this weak yellow guilt, dust off and ride into town for supper. Just another day's work. Let the grass grow tall and someday you'll forget it ever was. So cut the memory loose and go. Be done with it. Time will do its thing and you do yours. No more backward glance, no more covering tracks. Free.

I drop the smoke and grind it into the dirt. Like killing a memory.

There's a wind up, just a breeze you feel when you turn your face to it. And with the wind a fragrance, the sweet smell of clover. But it's late in the season for clover, so maybe a flowering of the grasses, or even the early morning's moisture mingling with the soil.

Somewhere a meadowlark calls the day to order. A reminder, clear and uncorrupted. A pure, simple song, a handful of notes. The signal that time, that heartless bitch, has begun her march once more. I climb back on board and start the engine. Everything spins, nothing will ever end. Some other hand is pushing me.

A farmer's turn and I return to where I jumped off. Back on the mainline, heading south. Back with the plan.

THE PANHANDLE CAFE

Thank the guy who said 'count as profit each moment the Fates allow'. The one with the faun drawing his bath and the nymphettes bringing pitcher after pitcher of wine. You can thank that guy.

My big moment and I'm sitting in the only square of light for a hundred miles. Boise City. I made it some time before 7 a.m. and turned off the highway and pulled onto the dirt and gravel lot in front of the first diner. I swept in slow and casual and braked firmly, kicking up a puff of dust as I slid to a stop. No rain for months and none for sale.

I ran the windows down and listened to the ticking of the car as it settled onto the springs. Familiar, I had a ticking of my own going on, overheated too like the car and black, black oil for blood.

Somewhere the town dog is barking, filling the empty spaces. I glance at my goods in the backseat, everything just swell and covered by a jacket, so up goes the window and out I pile.

The Panhandle Cafe it was called, wide open and taking on the big morning rush, converted as it was from the front office of a motel that still lay in abject defeat behind it. A dozen room shamble rattling in the wind, nothing left, not even the memories. One or two windowpanes intact and the yellowed curtains flouncing in the solitude. Dancing now the last dance they wish they had danced. Maybe some teeth in a glass by the sink, waiting for the five-piece band. Room keys dangling from hooks by the door, draped in cobwebs and dust and the ghost radio playing "Jitterbug Waltz" or "Cry Me A River." And nobody brushed or shaved or shod in their Saturday shoes. Nobody. None of the old swingers. They all checked out. It was hotel sorrow alright, done up in mint green adobe, but I'd seen worse.

I parked beneath the Fifties motel sign with the blistered blue paint announcing 'Wigwam Lodge,' its neon lettering bent to the shape of a teepee no self-respecting chief would bow to enter. Inviting once upon a time, perhaps, to the cross-country traveler, lit up and colorful in the night or rising out of the golden tones of the prairie grass by day. Less festive to the drummer no doubt, tasting so soon another day's solitude on the road, the endless opening and snapping closed of sample cases. Cutting the dry loneliness as always with an early whiskey.

Standing a moment next to the car I keyed on the sign and waited for the motion of the highway to subside. No vacancy the sign said, and I knew the feeling. The effect of the road miles and booze and nerves could not have been greater if a saucer had landed. With spacemen. But I grabbed my cap from out of the car anyway, screwed it down and trotted on in. A little grease to put out the fire.

"Hop off the hay wagon Maddock and get some breakfast," I said.

I got the scrambled eggs with toast and hash browns and hot black coffee and was pushing the food round the plate and spinning the cup. Waiting to catch up or just waiting for the waiting to be over. I don't know. I finished the glass of milk and the hash browns but could hardly shovel anything down in the way of toast or eggs. Just that twist of orange they spritz things up with in the country. I was that fried. From somewhere a radio crackled with a farm and ranch guy hollering commodity prices. Coming from back in the kitchen, if there was one.

The other clientele were a couple of truckers and a state trooper, seated separately at these doll-sized tables to the right of my place at the counter. He was an item, the trooper, built long and hard and flinty. A gray cop in a green pastel diner. Shiny black Wellingtons and trousers with a stripe and silver sidewalls around the ears and the kind of head you could bounce a rock off of. His eyes were quiet behind narrow pressed lids, a horned-toad, dry and dusty. He wore a mean looking revolver but probably wouldn't need it. Just flick out his tongue. All the thousand miles that circled round was his range, his territory and he meant to keep it tidy.

He watched as I stepped into the diner and sized me the way a carpenter sizes a load of timber – grain, warp, cut, moisture, you name it. I waved the bill of my cap at him thinking, 'You stupid cop.' It was way too early for the once over. The truckers didn't care, couldn't be bothered. The one with the cupped hands stared blankly into his coffee while the other Joe was skimming the want-ads. It was a big drama, this cafe.

Shortly after I stopped twirling my food the counter girl waltzed over carrying the tab, yawning wide, covering it with her wrist. Reading my mind, she'd come up empty. Straight off the highway she was, God knows where, and not new to the drill. Still waiting for her prince to show and serving up hash between times to fools like me.

Chancing a look round she totaled the room and stifled another yawn. With her fist this time. Probably awake since four a.m., scrubbed and fresh but the mind packed with cotton.

"Say, this coffee is good," I told her. "Did you make it this month?" I was tired but could feel the charm bubbling up. The wise-guy angle came free with the highway.

"Oh God, I knew I was due another day like that one," she said. "Is there a full moon out?" She let loose a laugh and displayed a mouth jammed from one wall to the other with the prettiest white teeth and around it a smile that was wide and real. It hovered play-fully above the curves that rustled inside her starched, pink uniform. A real smile and just a little fresh and I figured it was good for a com-plimentary slice of cherry pie, the one from the Fourth that didn't sell. Just over a week now and plenty water under that bridge. But the moment passed.

"Chop wood, carry water," I said and handed her back her day as I stood to go, leaving a nice tip and no regrets, glancing around the room for the heck of it. I had a loaded thermos and a fresh car-ton of smokes and plenty gas in the car. I had booze and a shotgun and bundles of money in the trunk. A mother's nightmare, but a guy could go far and far was where I was going, so when nobody said, 'hey pal, why don't you stick around,' I pushed out into the morning, first bite of a new day. Number one of how ever many more I didn't know or care to guess. Maybe a handful, maybe more. If I could duck all the jumble I'd put in motion, it might be a long ride. I just might have a shot. Snake-bit you suck out the poison. Or get over it. Your one chance really, which is all they hand you at the door.

I stepped onto the cement walk, the old, green, wooden screen door clacking shut behind, and standing so and looking due east now saw a yellow slice of sun rising above the ridgeline that formed the near horizon. An eager sun, burning to beat the band and everyone hot to trot, greedy for one last fling. Except the pale spinster moon, overhead and fading fast, losing once again to the light. Her most recent go-round unremarked and danced alone and just a glimmer now, the last to leave the floor. Too late, too late, like an aging beauty lifting her veil - but she'd be back. We'd all be back.

Seven-thirty in the morning and seventy degrees already, the bugs just getting airborne and the only moisture of the day crawling knee high and laying down fast. Probably over a hundred by three in the afternoon. Throw in some Panhandle wind and call the sheriff. Or the preacher. For another dose of love or pain or death or sorrow. Or whatever else goes round that circle...

I gazed across the gravel lot at the couple heaps and the trooper's cruiser and the two tractors idling, the sound almost homey in the warmth now with the diesel fumes a friendly pat on the back. On up from there I took in a sky as high as you can remember, clear blue crystal all around. Just a single pink, dream-shaped cloud floating alone, hanging to no effect. Like wash on the line, waiting for Mama. It was tantalizing and for a split-second I recalled a youth and the kid I was then, the long-gone Kid Lucky, MIA. Remembered him down to the dust on his boots. Until that light sparked out and a vinegary taste began to seep in with its host of memories; but I wouldn't allow it in. I moved across the gravel and fell onto the car seat, sweating that cold, oily sweat that rolls down the ribs on the black days and tuned the radio to an early morning country show from somewhere near Amarillo. Where I was heading, step seven and last in my golden plan for life, that tired, tarnished scheme. I'd be needing both and soon I figured, a new plan, another life…like all the other old jokers, finishing fast but out of the money. Still, if there was a way out, I was bound to find it. I always had.

I opened the thermos for old times and poured some hot black coffee. I lit a smoke and let the door hang open. Just a soldier boy on leave, with no brass shouting orders and no particular place to patrol and no one waiting up with lights ablaze. Bombs away soldier boy; every other puff a three-day pass.

I smoked like that and stretched out on the seat and listened to a cowboy tune that was flowing from the radio, a real sad song about a guy that got bucked off, lost his way. Strayed and gone bad. Only don't count him out. He was on his way back, all the way to the top. You wait he kept singing, in the style of them ballads strum from horseback, with the phony clip-clop of hooves and the wind whipping the brush. I could see the session drummer with his blocks making like pony, and ma and pa leaning against the shed out back, bawling their eyes out. It was some kind of touching. God it was good to be back in the country.

A big smile as I flicked my cigarette at a bottle cap shining away in the dirt and gravel. Flicked it and watched it smoke as the man loaded newspapers into racks at the front door of the diner. What I was waiting for, the early edition from Denver, delivered by trucks driving through the night.

All that way for a quarter. And chock full of good news. But nothing about yours truly…

ALL THINGS ROUND
ARE STRONG

There was nothing in the paper, no news flash, nothing but the usual do-gooders and bargains and believe it or not stories. Somebody got wiped out by a milk truck, somebody had a vision. Somebody's dog went to France. But no cops and no robbers. No police blotter. Too soon, or else they'd put a lid on it until all the angles were squared, nailed down back to front. One thing about cops, they know where all the bodies are. We had that much in common.

So nothing doing and I sauntered back to the car, pulled the door shut this time and started it up. Not much left but to push on through, ride the wind another hundred miles of panhandle and buy a rest and a room in Amarillo. Keep to the schedule and try and not do too much thinking. Take a hot shower and pick up a six-pack. Ask someone the time of day and sleep for thirty years. 'Give the Devil his due, Maddock, he earned it,' was what I thought, but "time to feed the chickens," was what I said as I backed slowly from beneath the sign, rolled across a sea of gravel.

I wheeled out of the lot and stayed below the speed limit until the edge of town, following the road as it wound south. Nothing between Boise City and the Gulf of Mexico but a thousand miles of Texas. That and this young Native woman standing on the dirt and gravel shoulder of the highway, thumbing a ride. Done up in a black cotton crepe skirt and deep purple blouse, concho belt and sandals with a backpack at her feet. An Indian maiden with thick braids flowing from under a wide-brimmed felt hat, black to match her hair and circled by a beaded hatband. Not unusual for Oklahoma, except for the hitchhiking, which isn't done, and the getup, which had a Taos flair. For a moment I even thought I knew her. When I pulled over, she climbed on board.

"The names Maddock," I said glancing sideways and offering a little cheer while she settled herself and handed the pack over onto the back seat. The liquor bottle loose inside my duffel clanked but the shotgun didn't go off in the trunk. Good medicine I figured.

"I'm Sara. Are you going as far as Amarillo?" she asked. She removed her hat when she spoke, revealing a young woman of much presence. There was beauty in her eyes, an afterthought until she smiled.

"I am," I replied and spun out in the dust and gravel and steered it back onto the highway and got it up to speed. We were traveling along a section of road that narrowed as it left town, somewhat dangerous with the line of long-haulers cheek to jowl and that bare, gray time of morning. She understood and we did not speak again until the road went four-lane and divided a half mile farther along.

"Thank you for the lift," she told me as the road opened. "I saw you in town but decided to keep walking. I thought you might stop."

"You saw me and thought I might stop?"

"I thought someone would stop and that it might be you," she said.

"That's a circle we went round, no?"

"Yes," she answered. "A kind of one. All things round are strong we say. It is how one makes great distance." She nodded at the wheels of the automobile and her gaze left me for the side of the highway, for the grazed and cultivated land, prosperous and open, spreading broadly away. Beautiful, hard-fought ground. For several miles on we said nothing and when she spoke again it was to a friend, wistfully, of times which had passed.

"...Before the fences our people came nearly this far. A band of them in our expansion. Traveling up the Canadian River, from what is now Okmulgee, in Oklahoma. My grandfather's father was a boy then and heard them tell of it. You know Okmulgee, Maddock?" she asked, as silence fell away.

"Been through it," I said. "My grandfather was a cowboy north of there, punched cattle on the One Hundred One Ranch. Before the land grab, when most everything still belonged to the tribes. He salaried at twelve dollars, tobacco and found and after a few years the 'found' amounted to over two dozen head. That's when he married my grandmother on horseback and hired some Choctaw drovers and steered them south to Atoka. The Choctaw were welcome and much prized for their ethic and the respect accorded them among other Peoples. The tribes were being pushed together some would say."

A true account, of which I had not spoken for many years. And more words than I had uttered in a month. Somehow Sara made it easy to come clean.

"He was called John Greenleaf," I added, proud of the common thread of his middle name. "A cowboy." When she merely nodded, I spoke again.

"We all knew him as Big Daddy. Are you Cherokee?" I asked.

"Choctaw. My name is Sara White Crow," she answered after a pause. She wove a silence round and through her words which I found enchanting.

"Big Daddy's wickiup was a Conestoga," I continued. "And along with the cattle they herded pigs, although I can't imagine how. It took them the better part of a month to reach their destination in the south, to settle in. Just over a hundred miles as the crow flies. Big Daddy had a deal with the local Choctaw chiefs and paid rental of a calf per month to graze their land. One hundred thirty years ago or thereabouts."

"He knew my people before I did. We are friends from way back," she smiled. "I suspected at once we were so. What else do you know of the country, Maddock?"

"I know the Guymon Salvation Army where I spent the night once, in the corner room with the trains passing so close the bed springs jangled, and the old bar downtown with the stuff tacked all around the walls. From when I was a kid, bumming with my brother. Before I went to soldiering. I know Lake Texoma on the Okie side and Tushka and Atoka and the Muddy Boggy. For the bass fishing. Even then most of the family still resided in the area. Most are at peace there now. I know little of the country that lies between."

"And this was your heartland?"

"A kind of one. South of San Antonio is where our heart resides at Momma's place, between San Antonio and the coast. Where her folks landed, immigrant farmers from the Baltic region of Germany, fleeing, along with assorted others, Europe and its wars."

"...My people come from north of the Boggy," she said. "Our heartland was the Canadian River and its tributaries, from Okmulgee south to rhe Red. Since before the Whites came and devoured everything like locusts. Our sacred home is further east, in the area of the Big River."

"You know your history well then?"

"We had no tv, we told the old stories," she replied. "The young have the outside world now and they are lost. Like sick children." Her gaze played upon me at some length that I might understand.

"You don't seem fearful," I said.

"The spirit is wounded. It is bad, Greenleaf. But the circle is strong and always returns. All things round are strong. This is what we believe."

"The circle is strong," I repeated in silence. Reverent, yet doubtful, allowing my thoughts to escape the confusion that for some time now had been their companion. Free as the hawk which, when circling the grove, held aloft by the rising heat, will watch his shadow fall, becoming one with those beneath the boughs. As if everything were joined. As if everything were one.

"...healing also resides on the circle," Sara White Crow said and nodded twice to seal it.

SARA WHITE CROW

"Sara White Crow was the name that found me, because my vision was said to be pure. A great honor to be a seer for your clan," she said.

"You interpret events? You see the future then?" I asked. We were making good time now, rolling fast through that stretch of scrub and sand that unfurls across the panhandle of Texas.

"...Not so simple as that. One becomes the future, only not beforehand. It is not clearly explained with words. Sometimes a dance or an offering is made."

"But you know who I am?" I asked, and there too I was curious. I also wanted to know. A part of me wished to believe that there were other shadows, not merely those that lay beneath the surface.

"...I know who you are. You are not a rabbit, yet you have the scent of one. I think it's the liquor. I smelled it when I stepped into your car."

"I guess I would say it's been a rough slide for me, Sara. But I've been roughed-up before. Just tired at the moment, I guess. I wanted sleep but I also needed the escape the highway offered, and those two don't play well together."

Spilling my beans to the Native girl and she took it easy and nodded. She could feel my discomfort, But I wasn't unnerved, more curious than ever.

"You mind if I smoke?" I asked and reached for my shirt pocket.

"Anything but kinnikinic," she said and laughed. "That stuff gives me a headache." She held out a lighter and steadied it under my cigarette. Then she turned my way and reached her water bottle over from the back seat and brought out my flask and passed it to me. I took a big slug without saying a word and handed it back and she placed it inside the duffel from which it came. I stared at her, tried to read her, but my wires must surely have been crossed.

"...Sometimes the medicine is worse than the cure," she explained. "Sometimes not. I learned that at Stillwater. I went three terms at the college there. The first in my family to do so." She was beaming at the thought.

Her smile matched in radiance the hard, level light of a morning which only now was lifting itself from the fields, slowly rising. She was a healer I sensed and of that I was sure. Natural and free, so that the path to her wisdom lay open before me. I took my cue and asked her a question whose answer had heretofore eluded me.

"I had this dream of a woman I was yet to meet," I said. "Never did meet, I guess. She was Anglo but appeared Native in my dream. She died before the dream, before I knew her, yet now I feel somehow

I must have known her. In this world, I mean. Or did she come to me only as a dream?"

"...It is hard to say, Maddock. She may have dreamed you. Sometimes that happens. Those you meet on dream journeys you will meet again, simply, as we have met this morning. She cannot speak to you through me, as we know, but it can go the other way. That is the future you spoke of."

I let her words flow by, never to settle deep, more like fast water on river rock. It came with a shiver though, a cosmic disconnect, like waking in the jungles of Nam.

"The way you say it sounds simple. Still..."

"...Once you are, then you must breathe. But not before. It is not easily explained with words," she said, as her gaze sought the peace of middle ground. I followed her gaze as we entered a wide grass-land plateau, a boundless golden plain, one of the myriad islands of high prairie that dotted the land. Home once, in the bygones, to nomadic tribes.

For several miles we remained aware, alert to the moment's promise. Two runners abreast, striding together across an expanse as wide and bottomless as time. Quiet and inward the pace, silent amidst the memory of a creation whose wisdom truth alone had sown.

A kinship flared with the silence. A bond of peacefulness, so that even the plaint of the automobile no longer sounded alien. Rather it was soothing, a welcome companion to the background of blue sky and brown and golden earth that rolled away beneath us now, awaiting the sun to bring on the light.

PALO DURO

We crossed the Beaver River and the Coldwater but by then we were falling off the tablelands, down into the country of dry river breaks and arroyos, the rolling, rough panhandle now spotted here and there with the pump jacks and small tank farms that follow the oil. That doleful country north of Amarillo, 'yellow' in the Spanish and named for the wild sunflowers perhaps, which blanket the region in their season, or the grasses that conjure an ocean of yellow in the frank, early light. Where the shine of the sun too, when illuminating the horizon, most often glows golden bronze.

Sara White Crow commented on the various plants as we ranged through the landscape and the different soils and recounted the medicines and fabric and utilities each provided - while I listened curiously, drawing a respectful blank. Just one long infinite blue sky, beneath which unfurled an immense stage dotted here and there with scrub and brush. But no story, no mystery for me; a simple and unremarkable stretch of ground. A cloud or two overhead, white as all get-out and silent in their passage above. Maybe something growing beneath it all, but you had to remind yourself and look hard to find it. Less always being more in the badlands. The dry quiet of sand and stone. A muted wind that seeks to howl. A simple truth.

Until you threw in the people. Until someone kicked the can. That sort of noise I liked well enough. Props strewn across the stage and every ham enamored of his lines. Fists and shouts and hallelujahs! rising to the rafters, while back in town the choir is straining to reach the high notes.

The big ball of humanity was the jolt. And a problem, too, if it found its way beneath you, the bodies writhing about, raising a ruckus. Next thing you know you'll want to dive in, straighten things out. A big mistake that soon or late always had me crawling from under the pile. My big love of humanity.

So you dust off and decide to sleep in, but it's rise and shine, the cab is waiting and they've started the meter. You'll never catch a break, buddy, ever. Except those one in a million times when you pass go and give it a rest, palm the dice.

My time swung by during the pause, and I took a backseat to it all, decided to go easy and had myself a drink from out of the bottle, but only a drink. I could have killed the whole jug, yet I didn't out of respect for Sara. That and I figured it wouldn't hurt to give it a think at least once this year, slip it in quick and get over it, the year being half gone already. Try the crossword puzzles sober just this once.

I lit another smoke and cracked the window. Seventy miles per hour and the purple sage wafting in and the vultures with their lazy circles high up like smoke rings and the ground starting to crackle.

"Gonna break a hunnert," I remembered the doorman say and thought back, barely a week now, to where it all began, wishing I could leave it all in the lurch and maybe I had. I made to reach over the seat again but held off and reeled my hand back and stuck it to the steering wheel.

Sara smiled and glanced over, humming and rocking, one calm unit. I looked out of the car at the world flowing by and everything was all right, I'd find a way. It's how people are. They want to live. A mere 24 hours since I broke rule number one, the heavy one, and here I was wetting my lips, ready to whistle. That's how lousy it can get. A numbing shame in that and something I hadn't counted on. Try swallowing that down when your bile is up the shaft.

Yet, I was determined to keep it down. I was running and tired of running and my blood had been sick for much too long. Though I felt a weakness in the wanting, I wanted anyway, to live again, somehow, knowing how little deserved. If only long enough to think, put some sort of mark to what had happened.

And then there was Marie and again I chose to live. Not so very much to ask and Sara had climbed on board to pilot me across. That was my story anyway, how I sold it to myself. That or she dreamed it for me.

Sara White Crow. A cloud walker it turns out. A bridge. A gift from Salome, the dead girl in my thoughts, straight out of dreamland. All these pieces coming together, all my ghosts, the living and the dead, offering themselves up. Sometimes you get better than you give, and I never received a better gift than Sara's. She let me stand for a time in her simple world.

As we continued south, crossing the Palo Duro, she spoke once more, in a wistful tone this time about her people, that they had traveled this distance to witness the cave paintings. So many grandfathers ago she could not count them. Their welcome did not reach so far, and they had stopped short in their quest. But she had reached this far, she had seen the paintings, gone into the park with the crowd of tourists. Paying her ten bucks. And thus, her people had journeyed also. She carried their eyes for them, and it was with a sense of pride she had done so. Another circle she said. From another time...

Fifty miles north of Amarillo we stopped for gas and to stretch, the halfway mark, one hour on from Boise City. Sara chose to stand in the sun while I poked around inside the station, tried on a couple of cheap straws and walked the candy aisle. I settled on a fifty-cent peco pie, the kidney-colored red one that sets you free. I sauntered out and stood on the gravel strip in front of the place, cracking down on the pie and stretching, thinking back to an earlier time. Watching the trucks crawling by, growling their engines. The ones I'd be passing again in five minutes. I gave one trucker a wave, to his sunglasses, the mirrored kind, and I saw him flash his teeth. Buddies.

A fine dust about belt high was hovering over the roadway and environs and I could feel the sun already hot and pressing hard on my neck. Waves of energy like someone had struck a gong or dropped a pebble into the cauldron where I stood, center of it all, frozen solid. Until the earth moved, and I came out of that one too.

"Should'a bought a straw," I remarked and pictured myself sporting a tall western style, about a 4-inch brim and tan to blend with the work shirt and jeans and boots. With brown straw worked into the crown, in the way of the Mexican horseman, a little foreign touch. Perhaps a ribbon hatband, cane colored and fastened to the crown by a metal pin done up like a branding iron, or some hat maker's initials. With a buttonhole tie-down to stand against the wind. A regular wrangler all right, with spurs to boot.

"Yeah, and with a horse, too," I snickered and dropped what was left of the peco pie onto the dirt and watched it cartwheel over the mound and gravel as the red ants commenced to scramble: a little red ant jig and lively as any tank town saloon. Each to his own I was thinking as I turned from the dance and headed on back, something definitely pulling my string.

Sara was off to the side in the sun, wearing her hat again and facing east towards home. She didn't throw much of a shadow. A willowy creature, small and slender in her black dress and purple blouse. The silver conchos of her belt flashing where it circled a nubile waist, hung softly on a young women's hips, the silver tongue of the belt following the impression of her thigh. I waited her out, stared at her from beneath the tin roof that shaded the gasoline pumps. One foot up on the fender, the other rooted in cement and gravel, I afforded her what time was needed and when she returned to the car and we loaded up she was beaming once again. A lovely flower, the first to open in spring.

"I feel strong today. If I had wings, I would be a hawk," she said.

She removed her hat and for a brief moment, I stole a glance at the band of beads that held the braids of her hair. Red and white and black patterned beadwork on dove-colored strips of leather. Diamonds done in black. Red triangles and circles. Symbols in everything. The earliest symbols, from just before Eden. On the beautiful, black tapestry of her hair, the young, beautiful ear. Some Sara I thought and flashed on Salome, my dream friend. Getting my women mixed up.

"Yes, and I feel less and less the rabbit," I told the young flower.

"You are not a rabbit, Maddock, though you run. But the rabbit does not often die of old age and there you are alike. It is the fate of many," she added, nodding twice to seal it. "And often honorable."

"Well, we all gotta go," I reminded her.

"My father would say: 'Do not simply breathe but fill your chest.' More firewater?" she offered me with the coyote's grin.

"And Big Daddy told me not to push the river, just ride it. So yes, don't mind if I do."

THE CIRCLE

It was early as we rolled off the high flats north of the city, out of the scrub and glint of sand and the first thing we see is the downtown, only it is not the tall buildings of downtown we had imagined but a grain silo, three of them, tall and white and masquerading as something they were not. And still no city. After the straight and honest landscape, a trick, a reminder. A clear note to those who would listen. But seldom do we listen.

I was basking in the good fortune an hour can bring. Giving Sara a lift, just riding together the seventy miles or so had taken me from dead-end case to one mile high. Her presence. Or maybe just the rising sun. I might have got there anyway, coasting down the prairie on a river of juice, burning in the glory of package liquor and nearness to the everyday divine. It has been known to happen. But Sara made it real, kept me distracted long enough for some healing to begin. She deflected my mind, lifted it from beneath a quagmire of troubles. And never spelled out the least of it. A simple, spiritual dimension enveloped us, in the way dawning light in a clearing reflects all around. Bathing me in a sort of well-being. She cast a kind of quiet around everything and shared her faith, which amounted in large part to a peaceful inevitability. The kind of faith that's easy to swallow and I drank my fill, quenched a thirst that rose deep from within. And like an ace bartender, Sara set up another:

"You haven't spoken Maddock. Only of the girl and the dream. You must tell me where you are heading, your home, so we may walk together some."

Sara's question spoke to honesty and trust, fine friends those, though trust was poison to my game. Truth however, a certain kind of truth, I had no fear. The kind of truth you discover laying between the lines.

"I keep hearing this sound, Sara, of waves crashing ever to shore. When first I dream and when I wake in the morning. It helped me through the recent times, some very hard times, this sound of waves crashing. I'm going to where the first waves crash to shore. It's what I give myself."

"Water is always a good dream."

"I don't know how this one will end. But I'm taking the straight line," I told her. "As near to this moment and where the highway and ocean converge as I can reach by driving. The only thing I figured to do. I'm hoping it will be enough. Or the start of enough…"

Sara nodded in silence.

"…I want to put my toes in the sand along some stretch of beach, the more desolate the better - that old story. I promised myself that much. I needed something to shoot for," I added and winced. Along the way I planned to stop at our old homeplace, the family farm, tie the now together with an older time.

"...afterwards, I don't know. Whatever part of me doesn't want to move along is welcome to stay." A long shot, I suppose, this glimpse into the future, but long past time to flesh things out. I hoped that putting it into words might serve to guide me.

"When I'm good and washed clean I plan to roll east along the coast, the Gulf, taking whatever time I need. When I run out of land, I'll wade into the Atlantic. I may drive straight through, I may start a family. The point is, I'm on furlough from my former life, Sara. It's a free ride from here, the ticket bought and paid for eons ago, though I'm still paying, I guess. I don't believe I'll ever stop paying," I said, and suddenly I felt the weight of it.

"And you go south because it is downhill?" Sara asked.

"It's the ocean...where everything begins. There's a girl waiting there, a woman named Marie waiting at the end of it all. A good thing if I can find the handle. Along with my business, which I need to breathe some life into. And one more trip around the wheel. One more spin. I believe I bought that at least. But maybe not. I don't know what's for sale anymore, what price you pay. I may have a few drinks on the way," I added, and I could taste them already, holding them down already, trying to, the leering, sick puppet tumbling out of his box. Making a lie of everything, bent out of whack, the way I always framed it.

"Now you are the one who makes it sound simple," she said.

"I know there's more to it...only that's as far as I see at the moment. I haven't exactly worked things out. I'm expecting to land on my feet as always. Taking a chance like in the old days when I still believed."

"...And seeing is believing?"

"I'll know in the fullness of time, Sara. We all will. I know that nothing good ever came to me quick."

"...The ocean, a woman, another journey then. A balanced vision. Can there be anything finer?" she asked while offering a sip of water. "And yet I see clouds, Maddock," she said.

"Lies perhaps? The whole thing a house of cards. Dreaming, all my life dreaming... how can you not know yourself? What is that?" I asked her.

"You say you were bettered. Has your story finished then?" she asked, laying the knife on the table.

"I never got around to the ending. I'm still looking for an ending," I said. "A nice ribbon to tie it off, though I've made some bad choices."

"You made some bad choices and now you make another. Why don't you wash yourself clean, Maddock? A hot shower is what the whites do - you don't need the sweat lodge. It is the right of every creature to cleanse itself. Then you can make your journey. Don't wait for the ocean Maddock, the tide may be out."

She smiled as she spoke thus, and when she finished her eyes were bright again and soft and this time she lit a clove cigarette and offered it to me. A big honor I guess, and I took it the way it was given, held the smoke in my lungs and savored it. I pinched the small, brittle-leafed cigarette and inhaled deeply a second time, as something passed, a shadow of light crossed between us. I exhaled and Sara White Crow nodded. I returned the burning clove to her and as she received it and tamped it out, she spoke.

"You will see, Greenleaf. It will be my turn to thank you next." She put the roach inside a coin purse that vanished into a fold in her skirt.

I gazed at her long and steady. Sara White Crow's world was free and soaring high, higher than the tops of the thunderheads that were building to the southeast now. Billowing sheets of white piled one onto the other, cinched tight to one another along the far edge of the horizon. A reasonable world, a simple world. Pure air and sunlight, a single path to water. All the colors in harmony, true colors, no one color lording over the others but in its season. Space enough for each note in the forest.

A world I had tumbled from, headfirst into a darkness as hard and flat and bereft as any truth.

Sara had come into my world to help my passage through. Sent by Salome, perhaps, or dreamt by Marie. Or maybe I was losing it.

I reached into the back seat and grabbed the jug and had a quick drink to put the stop on crazy. Sara, mercifully, did not glance my way this time. She knew this time I was drinking the poison. She merely continued to finger a string of shells and stone that had appeared in her hand while my mind and mouth were running. Hanging from the strand was a pendant of clay. A medallion. Another circle in a long season of circles. It drew my gaze. It was her gift to me. Her faith and her promise, as permanent as stone.

SARA

We were entering the outskirts when Sara White Crow asked again of Marie Halliday, the woman in my life. That other mirage in the desert I was crossing. While we entered town past the corrugated sheds and farm implement stores that were located on the outskirts. As we passed the warehouses and auto dealers and machine shops that served the farm and ranch community, before dropping off onto a frontage road and from there onto a main residential, following Sara's directions.

A quiet little burg once you left the Interstate. Hometown USA and hotter than a skillet at the diner. People leaning out of front doors and rocking on porches and screened doors slamming. The last cool of morning long since gone and coming way too early.

Sara pointed me to a small neighborhood park, with a mom and two blonde children playing in a pool of sunlight. The small boy squeezing his sister's hand as they whirled about on the lawn. The mother content with her fawns.

We stopped in the shade beneath a row of cottonwoods and I slipped it into park and turned off the engine. The trees were dropping their seeds in the early heat of July, crossing the hood of the car, floating slowly to earth like so many snowflakes, the ground around us covered with them.

The grass of the park had browned and where the children ran, grasshoppers clicked off in flight. On a branch high above us a cicada began to grind its song, and then another. Time too had paused.

We sat in the car and listened as it ticked off the minutes, sighing in the dark shade of the cottonwood trees. From somewhere there came a breeze.

"...Uncle's house is three blocks from here. I can walk it," Sara said and paused, respectful of the silence. She turned her face to me.

"...I wanted to ask of the one who chews your moccasins, Maddock?" She spoke demurely, as a woman might intimate about her sex. One part of my story had jig-sawed on her, the odd pieces, some of them missing.

"Her name is Marie," I said. "I met her a week ago. She hired on at my business and I liked her sense, her handle on things. She was capable. And she was attractive in many ways, enough so that I might have played the game somewhat longer. The job I mean. But I was through with playing, finished with all that, ground down to zero. Still, I saw a chance in Marie, maybe my last chance for something real, a chance to crawl from under the mess I had made of things, the sickroom I'd bricked myself into..."

"...But only with her, I realized. The way she arrived at the very moment I needed someone, the way she propped me up without my knowing it or making me feel it. I needed her and I wanted the luck she brought me. The sense she gave that it was okay, the clean break from my past was okay."

"Yours was an understanding," Sara said.

"An understanding I made solely with myself at first. But you never break from the past. That's what the booze won't tell you, the lesson if you would only listen."

"Understand, Sara. Things had gone so smooth for so long...I guess I became complacent. Everything came easy, no surprises, the money was good. I began to believe my own lines. And no one to give me a sideways glance, no one to make me think otherwise. Cloud Nine it's called, don't ask me why they call it that, but there I was. I slept easy. In between times I did my usual job and waited for the applause. I watched the money pile up and when I wasn't staring out the window, I was staring at the mirror. And I liked what I saw. No doubts, or just the regular ones, the momentary ones. The fears were manageable. A charmed life Sara, charmed in a way only the oblivious are capable of. I thought I had it all. I'd even kicked the booze."

"We believe that time is a trail," Sara said. "You are still on it."

"And now it has tracked me here."

"Yes. And yet your world was...simple. Satisfactory?"

"Sure. Everything simple. It isn't hard to get the picture. The hard knocks hardly came knocking. I drank from the glass slipper."

"Eventually I passed the routine stuff on to other agencies, took a percentage, gave the no-win stuff to the young guys that were up and coming. I was respectable. Nobody ran me, I was that kind of guy. Big smoke, you know, plenty of money. Friends called with tickets to the ballgame, women found me good company. I even found myself good company. Something was missing, though, slightly off kilter and I knew it. I felt it as plain as I feel this moment. But I let it slide, didn't want to look. I wasn't about to rock the boat. And glaring mistakes are often the ones we don't see."

"It sounds like the 'Long Summer'. It is what you call the veil before the eyes. Native people know that one," Sara said. "Remember 'The Trail of Tears', Maddock?"

"Yeah, well, somebody dropped the rock. That much I know. It came from twenty stories up and had my name engraved on it."

"Some circumstances are merely that," Sara said.

"Not this time, Sara. At the heart of it was a flaw. Pride. Arrogance. I carried on as though my good fortune was of my own making. I fell into that trap."

"A whole world locked-up inside a person. It sounds so human, Maddock, so lonely. Don't you often find it lonely inside? We look outside ourselves to find strength. In that way you become hawk and cloud and all the other things of this world. We join the Spirit, Greenleaf. We grow out from the soil."

"You're right about the one thing, Sara, my insides were a joke and no help to be found there and that was true. I started drinking again and a meanness I thought I'd buried began to dig its way to the surface."

"You lived for it," Sara said.

"That's right. One big feast," I said and looked away.

Outside of the car the Panhandle wind had risen. Black shadows of birds hurtling along. Brush near the gravel shoulder of the park were rising up, waving and carrying on like a bad dream. All the while I was thinking back.

"I lived for it. The way your people hate the whites and what they did to you."

"Hate is not the word I would choose, Maddock. All humans are on the circle. I might as well thank the whites for their greed, for filling the lands they fenced us from. Our desolation is a part of our strength again. We leave them their cities. We have the stars for neighbors."

"It did not work that way with me. I crafted a home of my anger. But an empty house once framed. And you can't go back. It's what I'm finding out now. Even though time leaves a trail, as you say."

"And now you've broken out. You run like the deer before a fire."

"That's right and I plan on beating the game. I'm willing to sacrifice the truth to live. Do you know what I'm feeling? I feel like I'm stepping into a crowd, Sara. Turn for a moment and I'm gone."

"It is not so easy, Maddock. You may have the strength for it. But I don't see you winning the fight with your heart," she said.

"I don't have your wisdom, Sara. But I pay close attention to the words. Another of your strengths. And I heard you remark that the circle is strong and unbroken. That is what I will hold on to."

THE CHEROKEE STRIP

I let go Sara near the corner of uncle's street and watched her begin the three-block march to family troubles. What was waiting for her, family business, the big problem being her darling niece, Leah. She told me Leah was in show biz at the truck plaza out on the Interstate, the Tomahawk truck stop, performing in a dance barn thrown up just far enough away not to be misconstrued. Unlike the ladies, who got misconstrued often. But far enough.

Gentleman Jim's it was called, and Leah was up in lights, packing 'em in. Her stage name was Autumn Dove, her routine 'The Cherokee Strip'.

When we pulled over at the park and lit up and smoked, I figured Sara was going to tell me thanks a bunch and read my fortune, wish me luck. The sucker's bet and I swallowed. With people it's never that easy.

Instead, Sara had prayed it seemed and *Hashtahli* had sent me to help her. She told me this. *Hashtahli,* with the long eyes. Out of her hands she explained, the gift she was laying on me. It raised me in her estimation, she said.

The favor she was to ask, not a small one, concerned the niece. Extricate Leah from the whites she told me, the bad whites that had traduced her.

"Right up your alley," she remarked, displaying her three semesters of college psychology. "*Hashtahli* sees both great and far," she informed me.

"All this time I thought *Hash...tahli* had sent you to help me across. I keep waiting for the road to straighten out. Is my karma shot, Sara?" I asked. A private investigator on the lamb seemed a fair definition of busted karma.

"You have strength of heart, Maddock. When you walk with us you weave to the fabric. To walk with the Spirit will be your great honor," she added.

Stepping out and closing the door with a light 'click', Sara moved round to my side of the car. She gave me directions to a motel across the interstate from the trucker's paradise that was cheek and jowl with Gentleman Jim's, my target. She would phone tomorrow, 'after the family pow-wow', she said and left me a smile and a gentle touch on the shoulder and then began to drift away. Just floated off. I watched her until she made the corner, down a block from the park. Like a dust devil, one moment and then gone.

So I backtracked and did a half mile of highway and pulled into the Prairie View Motel, part of the Colonial Properties chain, with coffeemakers in every room and a free continental breakfast for all the hungry travelers. Nine hundred channels on top of everything else and room service from the Rowdy Wrangler, the motel's four-alarm kitchen.

I parked on the side nearest the Interstate and walked past the pool, snug inside a horseshoe of buildings that opened away from the frontage road. All that good luck pouring out onto the god-forsaken prairie, with children splashing and running and a walkway through the lawn and shrubbery that led away from the rustic parking lot. A permanent barbecue grill and redwood tables with benches to round out the homey look. And a blond at the pool in a lemon-yellow one-piece, reading a magazine through dark sunglasses of large, round lenses. I made her for a Daphne or just plain 'Honey.' At home in a chaise lounge, real tight and curvy, looking for action in the middle of nowhere. Somebody's dog, probably Daphne's, was sniffing the chain link fence that circled the pool. A little white thing, all nose and curls. Mom and her pup and that long gone feeling of home sweet home. Tailored to fit.

The deskman, a late thirties guy and almost friendly, had been around. He didn't much care and when I asked him about the strip club, he said he wouldn't recommend it.

"You would not be very far wrong to imagine a cat house," he replied. "Though it isn't dedicated to that sort of pleasure, I'm told. More like a men's club, run for the locals by some out of town hard ass. Invitation only and all of that. Live entertainment, I believe it's called. The girls come and go. Once in a great while one of them will stay with us for a day or so. They're all pretty sad, really. Most of them looking for Daddy or think they've got a special talent or smile. You'll never find a cop over there unless it's to take in a show, work undercover you might say. If there's any trouble, you'll never hear about it." Having run the table he came up for air, gobbled some while arching a wild eyebrow that he aimed, along with a knowing look, in the general direction of the club. And all the while his nose was doing a kind of tango. It seemed like a lot of effort.

I asked him about The Rusty Wrangler.

"The Rowdy Wrangler. Stay away from the chili," he said.

I got the second-floor view, the one that flowed over the broad cement median and grassy shoulders and six lanes of concrete highway and up the slope, all the way to the truck stop city, sparkling like a jewel on clod-colored velvet. Thirty tractors and trailers, parked and some idling, loads of chrome and glass melting in a hot Panhandle sun that glowered from straight up already and plenty little ants crawling about the gas pumps and gift shop and cafe that baited the joint, which stretched a whole block until it gapped at the men's club - half-discreet, half-zipped, set off at an angle in the gravel. The glory hole. Sweeter than sticky buns at the diner.

I threw my suitcase on the bed and unlatched her and spread her open, flipped the gizmos and dropped the fabric panel. Ah, home the sailor! Any port in a bottle.

Then I threw the attaché and duffel bag and shaving kit on the bed and held the blinds back while I cranked up the air conditioner and turned on the TV. Ten thousand channels and I get this program about roasting chilies, a lame buckaroo with a ten-gallon grin and a butter and molasses belly launching into the exact way to do 'em; mincing and sniffing and fondling every last little pepper. A man's man, loose in lingerie, with a red-checked neckerchief and pink stubby fingers and knife cuts on those. Probably wearing spurs. More than likely a drinker.

"Better look out there, buddy," I says. Good advice, too. Might take it myself someday.

I pitched the flask with the smooth scotch onto the bed. But then I picked it up and uncorked it and had a real warm one, like swallowing a roach. I choked it down fast and then I choked another one, only faster and stood on the trap door, the twins hollerin' to get on up. A quick slap to get my attention and it worked, the booze doing wonders and such a bad rap, such a sorrowful rap. Maddock and his bottle - what an epitaph· "He drank until it hurt."

That brought me back some and I laughed free and unforced and stared at the framed art and wallpaper and the bedspread and golden wall-to-wall, the whole place done up in 'Autumn Splendor.' Leaves everywhere. Orange and brown for the most part, the color scheme it was called back in the Fifties, if anybody cared. Mind numbing the colors but still holding on out here in the sticks, which ought to count for something. We all ought to count for something.

With so much good news swirling about I decided on another plug and swallowed a big one. I felt it hit bottom and brother I was empty. Like a pail smacking way off there in the bottom of the well. Still, I was more edgy than hungry. And muttering. I was muttering something, some phony nonsense about the well never going dry. Just a distraction. I was buying time. I was starting to sweat again.

"Can the acting, Maddock and call the lady."

Thinking about Marie, wanting to hear her voice now. A big man again, but not so steady and cooing for Mama. And still fussing with the suitcase, wondering if it wasn't time to cut to the chase.

"Let her know you're on your way, Maddock. You love her, remember?"

I remembered. I pulled out a loose, short-sleeved cotton plaid with breast pocket. A tan and black and red number with a thin, powder blue line running through it.

"I'll dress early Sixties, call myself Todd," I said in a party mood and reached for the tumbler. A professional bowler if anybody asked. Any of that ocean of people that gave a damn.

"Welcome home, Todd," I told the mirror. "Long time no see. Can I get you a drink?"

I kicked off my shoes and emptied my pockets of the keys and assorted things, dumping them onto the little work and dine alone and die table all the motels feature. The little round one with the suspended lamp and four chairs for canasta. Dark brown like the carpet, so you don't see it until you stumble, whack the lamp with your head.

Next came the curtains and I cracked the window too and turned the air conditioner the rest of the way to high. I crawled on the bed and propped myself on some pillows and lit a cig and fished in the duffel. I had a 9mm auto and needed to touch base, like hide and seek. I smelled the muzzle, no surprise there, dropped the clip and counted seven, plopped it onto the bed and fished some more, pulling out a stack of hundreds, banded, ten thousand clams to a bundle. I had plenty bundles, twenty-five or thereabouts, last time I checked anyway and a wad of hundreds stuffed in my jeans. All that dough and no way to bake it.

They'll tell you it's smooth sailing, but don't let them kid you. It buys nothing. In my case, nothing to the negative ten, three points a kill and one thrown in for style. But I was free and clear, what I figured. Free and clear. Just a facial tic for laughs, night sweats and rubber shorts in case I couldn't contain myself. I was that kind of riot.

I clicked my way through the tv channels. Second time around and I left it on the ballgame, the Reds vs. the Sox. Middle of the 3rd, 0-1, a real barn burner. One more inning in the books, another life I could have lived.

'Take my place in line, mister, please…'

Next, I rang the Wrangler and ordered in, padded down to the canteen and loaded ice in a bucket and took it back home, where everybody was waiting: Mr. Nipper, my popgun, the unleavened stacks of dough and a killer view from the veranda. A view to die for.

"Make yourself at home, soldier. Reveille is at seven. That's p.m," I reminded myself.

And that was when it hit me. Amarillo was the last step in my big plan. I had arrived in Amarillo unawares and unannounced. Slipped into town with Sara and didn't know it myself, the mind being on hold. That old, gutless mind.

So, I proposed a toast and why not, it was my dime. Hoist one for the good life. Toss one down for all the guys at the end of the line.

"Here's to all the heroes," I said. "The little guys made of wax and steel. The charmers and the farmers - no two alike and good thing too. And let's not forget the ladies, bless 'em, with their cunning little teeth and those knowing eyes."

So I tossed one back, Kid Lucky getting his dose. Three hundred fifty miles from hell Kid Lucky was…free, white, and well-oiled. Off to a new start, a new love, leaving a barrel of broken hearts and a hundred proof trail of the bonded.

"Do you have to be that way?" I crabbed, flaming now, mocking now, the mind gone rouge.

"Dealer takes five," came the reply and I was left to wonder: 'Is this the bitter end of the old line...or the start of a new one? Is this what the bright boy bought for all his troubles?'

Why not? the mind offered with its usual sleight of hand. It plays a three-shell game, the mind, but I got them x-ray eyes. That's right, Maddock with the long eyes.

So I crammed my brain back into the box and picked the middle shell, wondering 'What'll it be? What will it be?' One more smoke and the liquor? Dancin' dolls?

Empty. She comes up empty. No punches left on the dance ticket, no swinging on the veranda tonight. Nada. Like a free pass or the ace of spades or the long shot at Pimlico, if you would only lay one down. But no dice this evening, the bank done closed, and the boys done gone…

So out go the lights as I pass the vanity, padding my way to a shave and a shower. Deep in the woods maybe but following the scent. Fixin' to draw from the well one more time.

ROOM SERVICE

While I waited for room service, I thought about this Sara White Crow and her proposition. I hand her niece a new life, no problem there, pimps being real neighborly, known for folding at the first breeze. She chants me up at the next medicine dance and we're even. Another variation on an old theme: Maddock the Chump. Only, as Sara says, 'It will be some danger later...but I see you making the crossing.' Like, in her head and I'm thinking 'With how many legs, Sara? How many broken arms?' I'm starting to catch on.

The way it always happened, sneaky-quick as a rabbit punch. Clients, intrigue, fall from the sky like rain. Before I have time to say 'no thanks', I'm banking the check, parked on the street or waiting by the phone. Like the spider and the fly. Only I'd get up and gaze into the mirror sometimes, a little curious, wondering, but I never turned a clue. Unnatural was all I could make of it. They took me for the wrong guy.

Ev, my Gal Friday, used to say it was 'inexplicable', which I never looked up. But after the first five years the agency ran itself, printed money. It got to where I had contract men all over the city, doing my bidding. I was just the banker. It was no end of easy.

The way it was with Sara White Crow and her problem. Even a Native girl, they tell me their story, trust in me, write a check. No charge on Sara, though, I do avenging angel for free.

My fresh new start only its déjà vu with a twist. This time all the ducks are lined and I got a full clip, I'm loaded, unlike my last life, the one that ended this morning at a truck stop in Boise City. Just lucky I guess the way the wheel keeps turning. I keep dreaming, sailing along until the knock at the door...

Only this time it's Jasmine, come with the big shot's dinner: 'The Ranger.' Steak and baked potato, vegetables, choice of drink and rolls. For an extra $1.25 you get the dinner salad. Wheeled it right in on a gurney.

I give her a nice tip, put out the cig and start to sawin'. It's been a while since breakfast and I'm famished. Got a lot of hungers to feed.

There's the one about running out, leaving it all in the dust. One of the older appetites. And there's the one about yellow, and the one about weak. There's the one about murder, if you count them as murder, and I guess you got to. That alone worth the price of admission. That alone gets you ringside at the big call to judgment.

There's the hunger for woman, brother and sister dog, and the one for thrills and the one for money. There's out of the mind, out of control, digit-x style hunger. And that ain't all...

Not even close. Don't forget *numero uno*, the laugher, the one they call life. You grasp that one with your teeth. So fundamental you've forgotten it's there, life, until it seeps away. Maybe you even pulled the plug, knee deep in tears. It's cause you love mankind...

"Can the analysis," I mumble and pour a tall, amber-colored scotch on ice. A big one, cool and clear as water coursing over rocks. I drink it down and powder my lips. Just like a gentleman... like a Gentleman Jim.

I ring the front desk and ask them to buzz me at 7 p.m., sharp. I got a date at the men's club with the Gilhooleys.

And then I lay me down to sleep.

THE BEAT DOWN

In the dream Sara was telling me to shake a leg, get moving. 'Time to feather-up, Maddock. Time to paint your pony,' she says. I got it but couldn't quite square the picture with the deal. I was some kind of drugstore chief in my dream, with neon feathers and a campfire and a bow I kept trying to sling over one shoulder and then the other. I was hopping from foot to foot, shaking a rattle.

I had a tent, no stately teepee, but a kind of pup tent, with horses grazing outside, a pinto and a palomino, from the withers down anyway. I could smell bacon too and watched as a pair of leggings walked past the flap. There was a big hubbub outside, and I gathered it was just a bunch of braves jabbering and told myself to forget it and dive back under, but it was too late, kaput, say 'Hi yo, Silver' to dreamland.

About that time they handed my body back in pieces, starting with the head, dense like raw liver I suppose, I wouldn't know, the mind being thick and useless. Or top loin possibly, New York style, about as dead except for the throbbing.

"Hello head," I blubbered into my pillow. "Long time no see."

Seems I mixed my drinks, got in bed with the twisted sisters. Took that long walk down Shady Lane, on the path to some midnight Mass. Dark, heavy wool on a dark and heavy night, with the wind blowing cold and the leaves chattering like bones. Next thing you know they're shoveling dirt onto your box and I'm squirming as it rains down hollow on the lid. 'Rat-a-tat-tat, Maddock, time to meet your maker' the clods are drumming. I kick the sheets off fast just then, like kicking the milk pail.

Somewhere in another room a motel shower is groaning, sounding reveille or taps. A lifesaver, cast into a hopeless sea. Little Ahab and the blinding white headache, bobbing off the stern. It brought me part way back, the image, the sound. It was something, anyway. One glint of something.

"Ten hut," I bubbled and lifted my mouth from the pillow. There was a cut at one corner and a dark brown splash of blood on the pillowcase, where it had lain. The opposite corner was also smashed, the tongue lolling about, off its leash, probing, thinking on its own.

I swung my legs off the bed and propped my arms. The world was spinning drunk and I was dry, no contents, my retching the hoarse, sorrowful barking of a dog.

"Shit fire," I sputtered, and it centered me for a moment, just a moment until I whirled away, off the ceiling, a perfect loop. I landed soft and giddy like a Ferris wheel.

"Easy," I said and took off again before I brought her back down to bed.

I lay for half an hour after that, long enough for most of what it was to come back to me. Trying to figure out what they had slipped me. Lying there like a city slicker, fresh peeled by the gap-toothed town folk. Or the rat-faced boy, making his nighttime run to the market. Pants down on Main Street.

I started to call room service for a drink, but the thought sent a crack running over my skull, crashing somewhere behind the right ear. A trembler. I closed that eye, one was plenty, and turned to the bedside table, seven a.m. by the clock. Time and its gay little wings. I lifted the phone and punched the number for the front desk.

"Any calls?" I asked the deskman in a croak.

"No sir," he says. "How you feelin' sir?" he says.

"I got one eye open, the color of a cocktail cherry and it's burning. Why do you ask?"

"You were plenty wasted. A big Injun' brought you in and dropped you off in the lobby last night. And I mean dropped you. About 1 a.m. I thought you two were drinking buddies."

"We are now," I said. "Have them send up some coffee and eggs and coffee, would ya?"

"Right away, sir," he says. "Anything else, sir?" he says.

"Yeah. Tell 'em to shoot the dog," I says.

I hung up then and wrestled through my goods. Guns, ammo, money, whiskey…all there. I headed off for shower number two, not thinking about it. I didn't want to make something out of it, the banner year I was having…get myself all gummed up in time.

BUSTED KARMA

Maybe it don't happen that way for everyone. It was never that way for you, just a dream and you haven't awakened. You're falling all right, sliding down glass and the fingers won't hold. You're yelling but no sound will out, the mouth open, straining.

It's bad brother, all the exits are blocked. They're coming for you to wipe you out. All you can do is wait for them, hands tied, shoulders, gagged, just wait for them and sweat. You're bawling like a calf in a wide, lonesome prairie. You're gonna drown in your own fear.

Or maybe you wake up numb as an eel, the color of leaves, somewhere in some jungle, stone cold sober and your trigger finger, the clit finger, already limber, the first one up.

'Maddock, sir and his fucking finger, reporting for duty.'

Like a maggot, wriggling with life. Everything smells sweet, all the rot and decay. It's a warm, wet, gauzy dream, and you're an army ant chewing through the stalks, red and black ants marching single file. Water, water everywhere and the birds don't sound like home, they're ratting you out. Easy to die there, melt away. Except for the spring inside, the one that never comes unwound. Rusted but trusty, it jerks you awake.

No? You don't remember?

Try the Texas Panhandle then, a holiday barn on a holiday road, all tarted-up for the weary traveler. You wake the morning guilty as charged, a bad taste in your mouth, like smoker's hack. The copper flavor of busted pipes and you swallow it down hard. You've won the lotto on Nut World and take it in stamps. That kind of smarts...

Laying over the right temple is a welt, like a knot of hard rubber, about a 10 1/2 medium. You can hear the blood flooding in, fixing you up, pumping into the gash. Getting you ready for round number two. And it hurts bad, bad enough you almost wanna smile. Only the mouth is throbbing from one end to the other, a swollen, purple, lopsided sea.

Down around your breast pocket there's a dull ache and somebody kicked your hip so hard its frozen straight. Why, them boys didn't even use their fists. Hard-luck farmhands from roundabouts, too dumb to join the army. They really gave it to you, they did. Payback for all your messed-up, busted karma.

"Excuse me?" I says, the lights beginning to bore in.

'Them nice boys from Gentleman Jim's. They dusted you off and planted you face down in the washroom, the pissoir, amigo, and now you owe 'em. You remember don't yah? And what *was* they thinking? Roll the old coot and shake him down, take his pride? Now I am smiling. A couple bad months, you forget what a kick life can be - until revenge comes along, that old pick-me-up. Like a sleigh ride, revenge.

And it's only your first night out, what a waltz, what an absolute wonder, only it isn't night, you tossed that clock away, about 500 miles back, and you ain't got no clock no more. You pissed it down the wishing well, into your reflection, the old you, right in the *bouche*. Remember?

So maybe roust yourself and pick your poison. Or cut and run and why not? Out the side door suitcase flappin', and don't you never look back. Or maybe belly along to the car like an inchworm, taking your bloody time. You may even find the answer once you crawl inside.

Only you don't owe them nothin', Maddock. It's all a big mistake. The Injun gal made you lose your bearings, come unglued and now you're out of bounds, dog free and taking chances. Your dance card was full without her, so maybe wise up and take a powder.

Trouble is, it's going to be a rough landing either way. Somebody else has rolled your chute and it's soggy, wet, and tangled; wind howls past in black and white and stone-cold gray tatters, and it's an awful long way to the bricks.

You thought you had it fixed, smart guy, the thin part you hoped to file away, the guilt part, sharp as a razor. Trying to hold it down, save it for a rainy day, but it's coming now, you can hear it now, just around the bend and it's coming closer. It's the whirring sound of a grinder, only darker, leaner, meatier. Blood and feathers everywhere, all the way to the ceiling and hallelujah on that.

So mix a drink, as long as it's straight, and toddle over to the mirror, Sport. Take a gander at the new you, real *suave sans cravat*.

The new you that ain't looking so grand. Pale and haggard, like in the movies. Only this one ain't showing yet, and you don't never want to share it, the playbill I mean.

So take a shower and come out clean. It's what the little Native girl told you to do. It's part of the great plan and why not, you've been begging for one.

Hashtahli is watching you, boy. You've been chosen. So wash them hands and come out clean. Or pray for rain beneath the eaves, head held high and mouth wide open. Or simply, bow your head.

LAVON

After the shower I threw on jeans and lay back on the bed and turned on the tube. I was dead tired from slapping myself around and split wide open from the neat little thrashing they gave me at the strip club. No heavy lifting for a while.

I spun the dial and let it ride, coming to rest on the local weather. They had the eye on some farmer and he was having bunches of bad luck. They were shooting the news spot in a plowed and dust-blown field that spread out forever, stretching over the horizon. Not a green thing for miles. The farmer had taken his hat off and was rubbing his neck with a red handkerchief and you could tell it was hot as hell. He looked like a guy with a large family to feed and nothing but beans in the cupboard.

He crouched and scooped some dirt and it was plenty dry all right. Everybody watched as he poured it down a wide crack in the soil. The news guy was antsy now…hot and gettin' hotter. Probably late for the early lunch.

"Waiting for rain in Conway, this is Channel 7 News," he says and then he says, "Back to you, Erica," and next thing you know there's Erica, a one hundred percent looker, pressing hard in a red sweater and gold danglers. Erica - always available, always reliable Erica. Sitting next to her the sports guy has the five o'clock shadow and it ain't even 9 a.m. He's boiling with hormones, radiating.

"Don't give it away, Erica. You gotta fight it, kid," I tell her.

I light a smoke and can the tube and mix a bloody. No juice in this one though. A bloody virgin and I'm staring at the old fork in the road. This day could go any number of ways, all of them bent if I keep gunning the hot sauce. So I call room service and order up a pot of coffee, some sweet rolls.

"Ma...I'm gonna go straight," I tell the girl when she knocks on the door and hands things through. I give her a five. Everything's picking up steam.

I get the deskman on the phone again, real nosey and helpful, ask him a couple polite questions about the Indian fellow and the weather and the price of barley. I thank him and pour more coffee and start smoke number nine. I got this itch between my ears.

While I'm scratching, I dial out to directory assistance, long distance for Espanola, New Mexico, down Santa Fe way. I'm on the trail of something, keyed up.

I write the numbers on a pad and sit back and give it a second thought. Don't wanna jump the gun going down that road. I give it a half hour or so of second thought, with Padre Island as the bait and sand in my toes, careless and carefree. Just a thousand miles farther along, at the end of some pier. Rum drinks al fresco with the little paper umbrellas and dancing the tango 'til dawn. Candles on the tables, the flames dodging high and low in a warm Mexican breeze. Shadows of palms swaying to the combo playing cool jazz, the drummer brushing his high hat. Gulf water lapping the pylons in some cosmic romance. And all the women of the island desperate, waylaid by the storm, looking to lose themselves and I'm their daddy. A scene I play in silhouette, darkly, from behind the veil, that old parlor trick.

'We'll blend right in,' I whisper and nudge my lying self.

Over against that, I have the Indian girl and Leah the niece and my Indian drinking buddy and a score to settle with the local yokels down at the strip joint. And don't forget Marie. Against all that we still have Marie, the third leg if ever there was one.

Amarillo just a way of saying I made it, for a time at least, a little pretend that I made it, dodged murder one. Come Amarillo the plan had been a long drive southeast to Florida and I looked forward to it, the chilling-out drive to a new life and high times with the girl. Putting some dust between now and then, a sidetrack to the home-place, maybe. Just taking the slow boat, the coastal route, wending my way along the Gulf while holding her close in the back of my mind, in reserve, always the hole card. Drop the coin and ride the drugstore pony, I tell myself. And you love her besides.

"You love Marie, remember?" I ask and nod yes.

Every fiber telling me to check out of this hutch and hot foot it to Delray, sweep her up in my arms and carry her into the surf. Like a promo, a dream moment. Instead, I lift the phone and dial her number. I clear my throat and wait anxiously as it rings through.

Marie surprises me. She doesn't pick up, the call is routed to an answering machine, her voice asking the caller to leave a message. It says, "You have reached M & H Investigations. Please leave a message for M & H and we will return your call as soon as possible."

I let her voice trail off, the message rattle around awhile in the silence. That woman kept the fire stoked, I'll say that for her. So now it was Maddock and Halliday, clever and why not? Marie wouldn't sign on for less than life. It's what drew me to her. Besides, a guy could learn something about taking a cut from that girl. I figured it was high time to take my swing.

"Marie," I told the recorder, "It's Maddock. I'm in Amarillo, playing cowboy for a day or two. I may have run into a little business and then I'm back on the road, heading your way. I'll tell you about it when we talk later...M & H, I like it. I like it a lot."

"I love how you're taking care of the business, following the plan. How you have your eyes out always, on the lookout for both of us. I'm thinking about you all the time, too. I already miss you terribly," I said.

I left a phone number for the motel and let her know I'd be hanging around most of the day. I told her I loved her, and the words felt like a jacket cut narrow in back. I'd get used to it I guess, or we could chase the feeling. I'd wear it if I had to and just like that I was tight with the girl, in step with the plan. Call it the power of two, it helped me get level.

Next, I dialed the number for Lavon, my old buddy, a couple hundred miles west in New Mexico, a straight shot on I-40. A straight shot to the straight shooter. I needed Lavon's help and he owed me one. Probably as much as I owed him. So I called the one and only motorcycle listing in the area and hit the bull's-eye.

The call rang through and the guy on the line said, "Apache Cycles, this is Lavon."

Funny, it was the precise moment I realized we were gonna do it, Lavon and me, extricate the little dancer. It tripped me up for a second and I came on all business but couldn't help smiling, dialed-in already, anticipating the action. Some local boys owed me big time and I wanted payback. I deserved what I got maybe, but so did they and I wanted them to be right with the world. That and I suspicioned there might be a dose of wickedness left in Lavon. I was curious to turn it loose.

"I'm looking for a '54 knucklehead block," I said.

"They don't make 'em, chief. Try the laundromat," Lavon said.

"Hey Lavon. It's Maddock. How you been boy?" All warm and fuzzy, the way you get with a long-lost friend. Lavon and I went way back three, maybe four days now, around the time he wedged a boot in my mouth.

"Well, this is a surprise. Don't tell me you're callin' the loan?"

"It wasn't a loan, Lavon. You earned it. As a matter of fact, I want to hire you for another job. There's big money in fighting crime. Or haven't you heard?"

"I'll tell you what I heard, ole buddy. I heard they're still looking for you. It's what my old lady said when she told me she'd had enough of my kind of luck. She drained four thousand of the five you gave me and went that-a-way. Drained it right from the account."

"Decent of her to leave a thousand," I told him.

"It's in my pocket is why," Lavon said.

"Sorry to hear that Lavon."

"I ain't. I got off cheap. What she needs is a bad-ass biker and I'm going the other route. So tell me about the money, the job. It seems I'm short again and lacking the necessary skills required here at the shop. Like standing counter for eight hours."

"A waste of talent, Lavon. I need you maybe two days max, pays three thousand and I supply the tools. No heavy lifting. There's even a retirement plan. But what's this about them looking for me again?" I asked. A crowd of little hairs were tap dancing on my neck. I glanced around quick in search of the bottle.

"Two men, no i.d., very persuasive. She said they made my screwball psycho friends look like stuffed kittens. They wanted to talk with me, so they leaned on her, danced her around the apartment, told her she had a day to think about it. Well, they ain't cops so that makes 'em robbers. Means whoever wanted you gone is still looking," Lavon said. "Means I'm one step ahead of the posse myself."

"I never figured them to vanish, Lavon. I'll choose my ground if it comes to that," I added. Like a tough guy, listening to my mouth and amazed some at Lavon, tipping me off for a second time. A mild shock to the guts, I must say. I didn't figure to be running from the bad guys so soon, and maybe never, only from the cops and maybe never there too. Well, well.

"No time to take it personal," Lavon said.

"That's right, Lavon. It ain't a curse if they don't swing the chicken."

We hung up then and I set about arranging a wire of funds to Espanola. The code for the money was *Semper Fi* and Lavon said that was mostly true, thinking of his girl I suppose.

Then I lined up a bus ticket, had it waiting at the money office for when he snagged the three thousand. He'd wonder when he saw it was for Amarillo. Probably thought I was still in Denver.

Next, I called down to the Rusty Wrangler and ordered brunch and told 'em to throw a whiskey and soda on the tray with the eggs.

"Tall and wet," I told them and hung up. I almost smiled thinking about things. All that remained to complete the picture of an eccentric cowboy was a barber shaving me in the room. That and a midget

I pulled the bedspread back and there was the money, so I stuffed it one more time into the duffel and covered it up and put the auto underneath and pulled out one bundle and peeled off three big ones. The guys downstairs would handle the wire to Lavon.

Then I just stared out the window at the truck stop, like watching an anthill. Daydreaming until a knock came on the door. It was room service.

"Someday it won't be the help," I reminded myself. "You know that don't you? And they won't bother knocking."

All and all though, a pretty nice lunch. The eggs were maybe a tad over easy.

COOKIE

When Marie didn't call by noon, I gave it a rest and slipped on some loafers. I figured to take a drive through the city, get out of the room for a while. Snoop around, maybe put the collar on some rustlers.

After the car wash, I got directions and headed downtown to a newsstand, pulling to the curb in front of a whiskey joint called The Full House. Looked more like a flush, the neighborhood being on the skid for some time. The better weeds had up and moved. Made no matter to me, I liked the ambience.

A sign in the window said 'Help Wanted' and next to it was another that said 'Happy Hour - All the Time'. Which had a nice ring to it, so in I went. Strictly business of course. There's normally a guy with the lowdown living in the bar next door to a newsstand.

The Full House was no exception. He was at the customer side of the rail, where it curved over to the front window, his back to the bar and staring into the street. The cook...in a white t-shirt and smeared white apron, smoking a cigarette. He wore jeans with cuffs rolled an inch high. Black loafers from a Fifties theme park and white socks. An older guy. With the Amarillo-Globe spread open, moving his lips while he read. I left a stool between us and flagged the barman.

"Whiskey and soda," I told him. "And one for my friend."

"Make it a beer, Joe. Thanks, mister," the cook said and turned round to the bar.

"My pleasure. I'm traveling through, told myself 'Spend a buck, you're on vacation.'" I looked in his general direction, a little off to the side.

"Looks like you drove through a wall gettin' here," he said. Part of the dance, he knew I was fishing.

"Women," I said. "I stopped at the gentlemen's club out on I-27. It's a private club I see at the door, so I tell 'em I'm thinking of joining, want to see what's what, have a drink, I'm on my way. Well, I get comfortable and have a few more, next thing you know I'm 86, can't remember a thing." I look over now and he's looking at me and I offer him a lying grin.

"Anyway, that's my story," I say and watch him take his time deciding.

"I don't drink nothin' less it's got a cap on it. Watch 'em take it off, too. Specially that dive." He took a sip out of the bottle to prove it.

"*Semper Fi*," I said and took a drink of my own.

"Navy, but I get along fine with ever body. Even Jarheads," he said, returning my grin.

"The name's Maddock," I said. "So what's the story there at Gentlemen Jim's?"

"No story unless you stumble in. The name's Carl. Don't call me Cookie, okay Maddock?"

"Okay, Carl. So I stumbled in. What's the big deal?"

"Deal is, the skin joint fronts prostitution, drugs, half the other rackets from the Gulf to Canada - between Kansas City and Vegas that is. At least it's somewhere up in the organization. You walked into a beehive, Maddock. You must've played real dumb not to get stung a lot harder."

"If everybody knows, why they still in business, Carl?"

"Texas is a funny place. More worldly than many would guess. The general understanding is that man is a flawed creature. But always striving. It being understood that boys will be boys and some of them grow up to become senators. Texans don't vote for virgins."

"Drugs, Carl."

"Most of it comes and goes through the truck stop. All but the local weed and powder. The small fries. The cops keep a handle on the big boys and bust the locals. Way it's been done since ancient Rome."

"You get all this out of the papers, Carl?"

"It's a small corner of the world. I keep my ears open."

"What else, Carl?"

"Little Caesar lives on Mustang Island. Outside Corpus in a hotel and casino that launders the money and distributes the goods for friends of his from Central and South America. At least that's what I heard. For fun they cherry-pick the talent at Gentlemen Jim's and stock their little playhouse on Mustang. For the out-of-town big shots. Forget what the place is called. You might want to drop in and tell him hey. His name is Reece, I believe."

"What about you, Carl?" I ask, while slipping a pair of twenties under his lighter.

"I take care of myself, Maddock. See you do the same," he says.

Picking the bills off the bar he snaps one and shoves off for the kitchen. Navy all right. 'Loose lips sink ships' and all that.

"The joint's called The Mayan King," Carl hollered at me over his shoulder. "Hotel and Casino."

"Anchors aweigh, Carl," I shouted as he wheeled into the kitchen.

Me? I paid the tab and walked into the light. Next-door down was the newsstand, and I went for it, grabbed the Denver press. Seems there'd been a blood fest, a battle royal, good versus evil. Way it's been done since the very first stone, Carl would say. Shocking, the paper said. Heroic struggle. All the big adjectives. But I knew otherwise.

I crawled to my car and started it up. Then I just sat blank a while, listening to nothing, thinking back and it seemed like a century. Sitting in the glare and squinting to keep the sun out, until I remembered the ball cap and pulled it on. Just glued, wiped out, like when you roll boxcars, every last dime center table.

Which left me exactly no idea what to do next, if anything, but the car kept growling 'Let's go, let's go...'

So we went.

BACK TO THE SHACK

I took the long way home, out north past the amusement park and the municipal park next door with its slides and swing sets and monkey bars scattered around the far end like the cheap seats they were. Then on down the west side and through the commercial zone on the south end of town. Amarillo, Queen of the Panhandle.

I found a package liquor called Tuffy's Kwik Stop and window shopped for a minute or two before going inside. The tongue sneaking out, darting across the lips means you're thirsty. I'd been pretty good all day.

I paid and walked back out and sat in the car with the windows down and smoked. Parked in the dirt and shade next to the liquors, a light breeze starting up and the dust beginning to swirl. A thorny old mesquite scratching on the adobe building in the wind, and not a dry eye in the place.

On the seat next to me lay the newspaper from home, about as appetizing as a Cuban cigar on toast, so I dialed the radio and came to a swing tune, a little country station. Every once in a while, I offered myself some elixir.

"Well, let's have a hit," I would say.

I sat in the car just so and things went to drifting, seconds dripping off the minute hand, the traffic flowing past - a noisy flashing shallow river, boisterous, jumping the banks like time in a hurry. And in the midst of it all this awful calm I'd become. Thinking back on when a smoke and a drink in the shade, no rush, no tomorrow, was *mucho bueno*. A low-rent business in a one-horse town was fine enough. Wondered if I should have folded sooner, left the pot to the other guys. The ones who needed to win but didn't know why. Regardless the cost. The shiftless, weak ones with their dirty tricks and yellow eyes. Instead of staying in and playing to the last sorry hand. All those chips turned to dust...

"It's not too late to walk," I told myself. "You leave now you can still get away with it." Grab the girl and make a life of it, Maddock. Keep moving until the trail grows cold or dies altogether. Only never look back.

"Bastard's way out you yellow bastard. No time now to grow tail feathers and you know it."

That settled, I made a toast to something or other, had a victory nip and started the car, backed from under the shade and headed for the motel. I figured it was high time for an afternoon snack and a little siesta. Maybe catch the ballgame or watch a crime drama or check in at the lost and found. Or drop down to Derringer's, the dark little cocktail lounge that catered the motel. Manhandle the beer nuts and scrape up a date for the evening. Or just wave my gun in the air.

Kind of light-headed, and goofy as a birdcage. Drove all that way to the Prairie View, room 209, chewing my lip and leaning sideways when I wasn't upside down. Gnawing into the melon, straight to the heart.

THE BIG PLAN

The first thing Lavon wanted to know was what I meant by a retirement plan.

"What did you mean by 'three grand, a retirement plan and no heavy lifting," he asked when I called to say the money was waiting. Turns out he had already picked up the money and the bus ticket to Amarillo. But first thing he wanted to know was the benefits.

"If we don't screw up we get to breathe a while longer," I told him. "Otherwise, we get retired and pretty much permanently. A secret incentive they put into this line of work, Lavon, to sort of speed up the game."

"You're a funny man, Maddock. Three days ago I was stompin' your ass and now I get benefits. I don't believe it can get any better."

"Oh it does, Lavon, it does. You're going to carry a gun and help me smite some sinners. A handful of the flock have strayed and you and I, brother, are gonna show them the way." As plans go, it maybe needed some work around the middle. In the fullness of time, I figured.

"What do you mean I get to carry a gun? Just carry it?" Lavon asked.

"More or less. A scattergun so you can't miss. Cut down but legal. In case our dear brethren aren't ready to walk the walk."

"I'm beginning to think three thousand is kind of light."

"Absolutely, Lavon. I wanted to see if you were listening. Seven thousand and nobody gets hurt. The other four when we're finished. You just wave the barrel around. If we do this thing right, we'll all be home in bed by midnight."

"And if we don't?" Lavon asked.

"You won't have to pay the taxes," I said.

"The other four when I arrive. I don't want any distractions while I'm totin' a shotgun," Lavon said.

"Deal. Anything else, brother?"

"Answer me this. What do you get out of it, Maddock?"

"I get to make up for lost time, Lavon. Or maybe I'm off the clock. I haven't decided. Let's say I'll let you know when I figure it out."

"Money?" he asked.

"I bet there's loads of it lying around. We'll pick some up on the way out. Anything else?"

"Rent me a Chevy," he said. "I ain't riding back home in that breadbox."

"Done," I said and hung up quick before he got on a roll. Lavon was a bright boy, all right. One day soon he'd open his eyes. And when he did, I didn't want to be there.

LOVE ACHES

After the chat with Lavon, I cleaned up and watched the news and stared out the window. A little early for Gentleman Jim's, just a couple dark sedans. Not that I wanted to drop in, get my ears stapled. But the Tomahawk truck stop was doing land office. All sparkly and busy with row upon row of automobiles, shining bright as fool's gold in the midday heat. Colorful little gawky bugs hopping all over the place, backing their cars and calling out and milling around. Like studying an ant farm it was. Gasoline instead of sugar water. A wonder anything got done. Which reminded me.

I turned away from the window and stared at my own campsite, a restless pile, lost in the confusion of the bedspread.

'Maddock the big shot, holed up with his sterno and shaving kit.' Knocking myself for laughs and gettin' a barrel full.

"Could be worse," I managed. "Could be..."

Plenty worse. I might have made the long walk for nothing, instead of the presidential suite at the Prairie View. What it might have been under all this treasure of sun and wind, but here I was, zigzagging like a rabbit from out of a woodpile burning bright. Nice view from up here, too, better than three I could think of. Make that four, let's not forget Charlie, my own personal doppelganger.

'Wise up, Maddock. Not everyone went down in flames. And you

aren't the first cherry's been popped.'

"Wise up, yourself," I said. "Where'd you hide the bottle?"

I went straight for the clear stuff and dug it out of the duffel, tossing ten grand here and there getting after my booze.

"Money's wasted on you, Maddock," I muttered, draining a mouthful.

Lowlife. Jackass to a thoroughbred. Buy yourself a shave, big shooter. Take your money and float a dream with the girl. You and Marie on the Riviera.

'Maybe I'll do that...if she calls. Which now that I think of it... no, she'll call. Marie doesn't know of lies and deceit. That'll be my big contribution to the party. Showing the girl how to do it all wrong.'

"Why don't you screw yourself and get done with it. Yellow whore bastard."

On and on like that, Big Maddock and Little Maddock, having it out. And all the while I was pulling a folded knit short sleeve out of the suitcase, something casual for a cocktail at the little cocktail lounge. After 4 p.m. they lay out the weenies and dice-sized cubes of cheese with toothpicks and crackers and fruit and wheel out a steam table for the big taco bar. *Muy bueno*, Senor.

"You hit the mother lode again," I mumbled.

'Let me tell you about your mother,' I began as the telephone clanged and

I was saved by the bell, except I knew it was Marie and I hadn't polished my speech.

'Wing it, Maddock, or dodge it. Just don't drop it.'

"Hello," was what I said and that ought to have covered it.

"It's Marie, Maddock. How's my sweet, sweet angel."

"You must have the wrong room," I replied, and we laughed in relief, roiled about, waste deep in love again.

"So how is Amarillo? Got an oil well yet, Maddock?" she asked, and I could feel her smile. It came so easy for Marie.

"I got a whole field of pump jacks workin'. I got a Cad with longhorns on the hood and a deer rifle in the back seat. I got a case of Pearl with Lone Star and Shiner mixed-in, iced and waiting for the cousins. All I need now's the potato salad and some good lovin.'"

"Why don't you bring your party down to Florida, Slim. I got everything you need in my back pocket," she said.

"That's my heart you hear knocking, Marie. Only we may have to hang loose for a couple days longer, but only a few. I'm in the middle of some charity work for a Choctaw lady I picked up hitchhiking. Her little niece is in a jam, but I think I can un-jam her...anyway, how's the hunt going on your end? We found a flop yet for M & H or am I gonna be sleeping on the beach?"

"As long as you're not sleeping in a teepee."

"I'll sleep anywhere as long as it's with you, darling."

"I love the way you say that," she sighed. "As far as an office for M & H, I've visited several. I have three excellent candidates in three different but equally fabulous locales. They all have in common a second floor with balcony, because that's where I see you and I most evenings, side by side with the sun diving under. Royal palms and blue sky and the night's silver waves. All of them with a view of the ocean sand, landscaped and with feather palms everywhere. Oh, there may be a fourth, on the intra-coastal for the sunset, and they all have a trap door, in honor of the boss."

"Marie, if you think I'm wary, like everything's a snare, don't," I said. "With you I'm not. With you, things have never been so easy. I'll tell you someday."

"You don't have to tell me everything Maddock or anything. What's to tell? That you've been around the block? That you can take it and dish it out, too? I know who you are. Maybe I even know some of what you won't let on. But I don't care. None of that matters. All I care to know is, can you be a man to my woman? I may not be everything you think I am either, Maddock. But if you can find the way, maybe we can start fresh, from scratch, make our own love and pain. Just you and I. If we want, we can even invite the world."

"No one's ever made a better offer, Marie. Is it too late to accept?" I asked.

"Not for me, Maddock. It will never be too late for me."

So there it lay, all of it, the whole show, packaged and bowed and left where I was sure to find it. More than any person could hope. I shook my head and placed the phone gently back in its cradle. Kid Lucky. One more cut of the cards. One more trip round the moon.

LOVE HURTS

After I hung up on Marie, I took a shave and a shower. I let the water cleanse me, all the poison leaking out of my pores. I could feel it flowing away, a wasted nowhere river, circling the drain.

Say I played it loose these recent months...still, I always knew what the booze was about, the dark green bottle that filtered the light. Call the light truth if you must. It's your nickel. While you're making change, I'll have another.

But along with the booze, incidental to it, I spied a meanness creeping in. Partly the curveball I stepped in front of, the one life whips by you. Like a slap and you never forget, at least I never could, didn't want to and that was the ugly part.

I was always wise though, thought so anyway, but never really mean. Not until later and by then, it fit like a glove. The spare skin I never knew I had, growing just under and itching for the first skin to molt. When they killed my friend...before I killed them back...the outer skin slid away. I scratched it loose.

And I was comfortable with it, the new skin, only the eyes were dull, old eyes that needn't look to see. That was the tradeoff. The eyes took it all in, knew it all beforehand. Not the emerald, green eyes of the boozer, either. Grey eyes, metallic, cold, clicking eyes. Get-even eyes that never once startled. Three men had looked into them. The three dead wise men. I sent them over, knowing. They got to know the truth. Everybody gets to know the truth. You only need wait your turn.

"Tough luck all around, is that it Maddock?"

'Sure, sure that's right, but look at the bright side. It'll be real cheery when you quit gettin' stomped. Just a theory, but twice a week is a bit busy even for you. And that don't count the cops even, but never you mind the cops. They want to give you justice is all, it's what they deal, it's the shield they'll carry you out on...'

All that good news perking me up, but something kept hollerin' at me from down below, at the bottom of the hole. A faint voice straining to reach the surface, give me a head's up.

I dialed the number for the cycle shop again and they handed the phone off to Lavon. In the background I could hear some farmer rapping the engine on a hog over his mumbling voice. I spoke into the phone, to Lavon, but he couldn't hear me.

"Come again," he said and covered the mouthpiece and must have yelled something because when he came back on it was quiet.

"Sorry about that," he said. "Now how can I help you?"

"It's Maddock, Lavon. Just need a minute. Something keeps gnawing at me, begging the question. 'How come Lavon's broke?' and 'What happened to his pay for kickin' my ass?' Or did I miss something?" I asked.

"Don't know how to say this, ole buddy, but I did it for nothing. I owed a cop, and I did it as a favor. Got a couple of meals out of it, couple of drinks, and the chance to meet a swell, sharp little killer. You remember Enrique, don't you? Sort of tan fellow? Whipped you with that antenna and laid one in on your kidneys?"

"Can't believe you'd do it for nothing, Lavon. You told me it was all about the money."

"Well it wasn't fun, if that's what's bothering you. The second job they was planning, that was for all the chips, twenty-five large, but the first one was gratis. Some vice cop named Evans, scum ball, had me over a barrel. And I mean barrel, as in Glock. Caught me with enough angel dust to levitate a truck. He put me up to your beatin'. More or less volunteered me."

How about that. Me, Evans, Lavon, the whole catastrophe. A daisy chain of snakes, gnawing through their tails. A fellow has just gotta be more careful picking friends. Something to remember for the next life.

"It's a small world, ain't it Lavon," I shouted over the rumble of another cycle revving up.

"Gettin' smaller all the time," he hollered and it seemed like I heard his laughter. Made me want to tell him about Evans, what fun we'd had together, but the cycle roared to life, only louder this time and coughed once, twice, before the line went dead.

DAPHNE (THE MAKE)

Next stop was Derringer's, for the cocktail hour and mooch bar and socializing with the motel crowd. You never done it, you ain't arrived.

It was down a carpeted set of steps and off the lobby, sort of hidden, but I could hear the bottles and glasses clanking and followed it on in. Five o'clock can't come fast enough for the honest worker, but it was only 4 p.m. where I was and that left me, a waitress and the bartender. Throw in the kitchen crew of the Rusty Wrangler making a racket through double doors off to the side. Oh, and Daphne was there. What I called the woman from the motel pool. She was there also. The one-piece blonde from the swimming hole sitting in a dark cove in the corner, the whole place dark and cuddly. She was glowing like caramel, all sticky sweet and moist, expert hands cupped round a candle that graced the table of her booth. She was wearing her signature yellow suit with a yellow pastel purse that jumped right down to the yellow high-heeled pumps at the tips of her toes. Legs like the entrance to some all-boy fun park. Long and slender with a waxy sheen that ran beneath the nylons. Like chasing a firefly, only this one had landed, way off there in the dark.

I gave the room a quick once over and sure enough I was it, the big one and only. It didn't take brains to grab a drink from the bartender and double up with Daphne, make a big splash. So I waded through the tables and docked at the bar. You had to like my chances.

The bartender's name was Jeffrey. Middle twenties and real likeable. Everybody's pal. After a little chumming around he served me a vodka. Nothing special, just ice to get in the way. I asked him if he came there often and he nodded and chuckled and kept cleaning at his glass. A cheery sort of fellow. He had a handlebar mustache and gold vest and wore a garter on the right sleeve and looked the part. Real calm is what I'm saying. Took his time when he poured.

Over in a far corner the waitress was setting up for the chow, barely making a sound with all the ladles and silverware, trying hard not to break the spell - Derringer's, where the love sharks come to swim.

I sipped a quick one from my drink and kicked Jeffrey a five, spun round with my glass and dropped off the stool. I took my own sweet time shuffling over, Daphne glancing up as I made my way to her hutch. I smiled as I introduced myself and slid into the booth like nobody's business.

"You can call me Dolores," she replied to my introduction, "and I'm very pleased to meet you too, Maddock. What took you so long?" A wonderful smile, easy. And round it all the jukebox was playing Crazy Arms, Patsy singing her housewife blues and I couldn't conjure a word. I merely smiled at Dolores, saw myself in her eyes. It seemed as though we were two small, sad creatures and I didn't want to go there. Not this early.

"You're beautiful, you know it?" I said. It was true too, and even though we were these lonely creatures, it was a pleasure to tell her so. It caught her off guard, the way I delivered it.

"I mean it," I told her, and she nodded in an off-hand fashion. It was old ground for her, this beauty thing, a familiar path that had never gone much of anywhere.

"You're kind, Maddock. There used to be real gentlemen in this town, guys with a line maybe, but gentlemen. I guess I'm getting old, 'cause I miss the old days." She peered at me with soft, eager black pupils, the eyes glistening, the mind gazing calmly inside, recalling the good times, everything fresh and hopeful, youth and its lustful ways. Working her poison on me, starting to tighten the coils. I let her, like slipping into a warm bath. I let her have her way and there was nothing easier.

"You're not that cagey are you, Maddock? Nothing like the usual dusters that blow into all the honey traps along the interstate. Spruced-up and buttoned tight, drenched in musk or spice cologne, sporting those big shiny buckles and hiding under those ten-gallon hats. Wranglers all, just no saddle and no horse either. Drifters, looking for the next warm thing. You aren't one of those, are you?"

"Dolores? If I was looking..."

"You needn't tell me, Maddock. I'm not pressing. I know the type I fall for. It's why I never got clear of Amarillo. I like the dust and the wind and the guys cracked like leather. If I was the beauty I wished...but hey, I'm solid and I love my man. Makes you wonder why none of them stuck, though. Makes me wonder, anyway."

"Sometimes it's all in the deal, Dolores. When the cards are running cold and nothing left to do but push away from the table.

That's when you find out you're not alone. Sometimes as simple as that."

"You wouldn't think love was that hard to give," she said. "It's free, isn't it? I always believed it was, never wanted nothing for it. Just to get my share."

I didn't say a word to that, just smiled and waited a bit, a little ways out of my depth. When love came knocking, I generally flooded the exit.

"And I don't necessarily mean the flesh, Maddock, though I love a man's body. But bodies lie. It's the mind that hurts for love when all is said and done. It's the mind, finally, that feeds off of love. Well, I guess I've always been hungry."

"So have I, Dolores. So have I. But why don't we eat first?" I asked and slid from the booth while holding her hand. I was being *tres debonair*, trying my best anyway and she knew it and took my lead as I helped her out with style. She was game all right and fell against me laughing.

"Would you care to join me for dinner at the Wrangler, Dolores? I'd love your company," I said.

"With wine and the shrimp cocktail?" she whispered, her warm breath running lightly across my cheek. Glowing pleasure in the teasing, crawling my chest now and tilting the world.

"Why not? We can play big city. I can even take you home and tuck you in later, if you'd like," I said and breathed lightly into her ear. Like palming dice or passing cards. Setting the tone was all - chapter two of How to Bed the Ladies. She knew, she smiled, she nodded demurely, her lashes guiding me on in.

We gathered our things and took our time in leaving, making single file. At the exit I let Dolores drift while glancing back at my old buddy, Jeff. He was a picture all right. A Rembrandt say, only more discreet. Holding a tumbler overhead, gazing at the light flowing though, he was smiling. Like I'd filled an inside straight and he knew it.

Dolores, my conquest, stood aglow outside the swinging doors of the lounge, waiting patiently, holding her yellow purse with those delicate hands, dangling it there in front. Kind of a lemon yellow in the new light. She had her hip hiked up on one side and she was standing there with a bug-eating grin.

"You know I play for pay…right, Maddock?" she asked with a smile. The smile gone a little serious though, the corners at least, like she didn't care so much for the business end, the math.

"I was hoping so, Dolores," I replied. "In fact, I was counting on it," I said and brought her round by the shoulders and held her close in the light.

DOLORES

It was late when they threw us out of the Wrangler. Threw us out in a friendly way, everybody real friendly. The maitre'd joined us at our table and polished off the sherry with us and kept us in clean ashtrays. Dolores was twirling around like a flagpole sitter before they run out the net. A gone pecan if you never seen one.

We tipped everybody hard and spilled the red wine and cracked wise like navy on maneuvers. It was a blue ribbon finish all right, a mad mortal dash at life, the big brass ring. Nobody ever gave it more of a shove.

It wasn't real far and when I got Dolores to her front door, I put the mash on her like a teen angel, my hand caressing her breast, crawling outside her jacket, chewing her lips and leaning on in.

"You're a tiger," she purred and threw in a little growl as I opened the door. We stepped through and right away I knew the meter was running, Dolores and the Tiger, burning through the pin money. And why not? I laughed. I got plenty money so why not. Let's spread it around.

Dolores must have understood and promptly tossed her jacket on the couch, did a little twirl and sank into the cushions. She gave me a tender look and I felt something catch in my throat, a warning, but I paid it little mind. No one gets hurt I reminded myself. Not you, not the girl. Money for info. Nobody gets wet.

"I wanna play this one standing up, Dolores. You understand?"

"I don't understand anything anymore. You treat me like something special, a pearl necklace, all smooth and shiny. Something rich, perfect almost, like a prize. I'm just not used to it. I don't trust it. In my dreams, maybe."

"It's a dream alright, Dolores. But the bind I'm in, we're gonna have to cut through the dreamy part."

I put some money down, a couple hundred under the ash-tray on the coffee table. She flicked her eyes at it, couldn't care less. I mixed her a drink and made myself one at the wet bar and headed to the sofa. A very snazzy joint for high desert nowhere. Everything solid wood, high-end fabrics and carpet you could hide in. Drapes tumbled everywhere. Lead crystal decanters and five-hundred-dollar frames on the art. Made it all buckin' the broncos.

I slid onto the couch sort of sidesaddle and nestled on in.

"It's this Reece fellow, Gentleman Jim's I'm interested in. You've been around, Daph, uh Dolores. Can you help me?" I wheeled my arm over the back of the couch and let it drift ever so lightly onto her shoulder. It settled soft as a feather.

"I wanna play," she said. She was starting to fade, slurring a little. She was curling a lock, had it pulled over one eye.

"I do too, Dolores," I said. "If you're a good girl, I'll ride you like a bandit. The money's for information, okay? The loves free, remember?" I was losing her.

"I'll make scrambled eggs, toast, coffee. We'll have breakfast in bed," I wheedled. Okay Dolores? But first we need to talk."

I got up and went into the kitchen, rummaged away in the cabinets for the coffee, found it, started a pot. I peaked around the corner and she was nodding but vertical. A dream date like you never had.

"Have a smoke, Dolores, they're good for you," I hollered.

"I wanna play, Maddock. I wanna play cowboysh."

"Let's be professional, Dolores," I shouted from the kitchen. Then not another sound until I heard a tumbler clunk and ice rattle as I was pouring the coffee. I put it on a tray and rounded the corner and there she was, conked out on the settee.

"Strike three," I said and Dolores said, "Uh," and hiked at her skirt.

"Let's be sure and get our money's worth, Maddock," I said. I set the coffee tray on the table and pulled off her shoes and scooped her up and took her to the doghouse. I had a lot of questions for Dolores, and she was pliant alright. Maybe a little too eager.

"Tell me again about Gentleman Jim's," I said.

"Uh," Dolores said.

"Your old buddy Reece?"

"Uh," she said.

I unfastened her necklace and pulled the gold earrings off, rolled back the sheets and swung her on in. I pulled her blouse out of the skirt so she wouldn't bind and gave her a peck on the forehead. The little girl I never had, never would.

"Goodnight, Dolores, you doll. Did I tell you you're beautiful?"

I dowsed the lights and made it to the kitchen and turned off the coffee, cleaned up a bit. I emptied the ashtrays and set the crystal on the wet bar and straightened the couch. I kneeled to pick a pillow off the carpet and tossed it on my way to the door. Surveying for a final time the scene of so much wedded bliss – me, Dolores and the wonder years. Wondering at the small sad animals we had become.

I hit the switch and shut the front door with a mild sort of regret and right away I was looking for the moon. Judging by the wan light and the shadows cast, it lay somewhere behind the peak of the roof.

'Black cat spilled the milk' they used to say and I had to wonder whether people still drank milk, still looked at the moon.

"Don't matter where you are or what you're doin', does it, Maddock? It's always four a.m. and the righteous are snoring."

I continued down to the sidewalk and lumbered over to my car. Tired and ready to roost. With one last punch on the dance card, one last dime. With one last stop to go.

BEAR

I pulled into a narrow dark slice of shadow that lay between the truck stop and Gentleman Jim's, rolled to a stop and parked. If anyone asked, I was just a farmer getting his bearings.

I put the cafe and convenience store over my left shoulder and the strip club dead ahead and just far enough. Four cars sat glistening in front of the club after hours; two foreign sedans, a monster pickup and a coupe de ville. Over my shoulder a car now and then rolling in for gas or coffee, somebody piling out to stretch or take a leak. It was straight up 4 a.m. but nobody stopped the presses.

Outside of holding my lids open and yawning them shut, I stared at the boy's club and the boy's club stared back. In between all that excitement I counted the sparkles of glass lit by headlamps sweeping the parking lot. Added them up and put them in my little bank of memories. All the little sparkles from all the broken bottles scattered over all the stinking lots I spent my life in. I smoked too and had a nip to hold me and let the warm feeling flood over, the feeling that a stakeout four hundred miles from home was almost home, or close enough.

Near as I was going to get anyway. Familiarity doing its thing, the old rhythm of watching and waiting as soothing as a lullaby and making me almost dreamy. One more night in the doghouse, but at least it was my dog.

I turned on the radio and stared into the glow, like the center of everything, the absolute center of nothing. Twisting the knob, the way a sleepwalker twice in his dreams. To rest my eyes, I looked east now and again, out into the dark black prairie. Once or twice a reflection, a pair of glassy eyes stared back my way. Hungry eyes. All the critters roaming about, looking for snacks.

Through the windshield I could see a smattering of stars twinkling in the distance, scattered like a spray of diamonds on deep blue velvet folds. I ran the window down and could just make out the low rumble of diesel engines, over on the truck side of the plaza. Wind too, gypsy wind rattling whatever wasn't tied down and blowing my way.

Twice I got out and went to the self-serve for coffee and a sweet roll. Beneath a moon that was up there now, near the top and sailing over. Clouds too, like horses racing and near enough to touch. Beauty in everything.

I had another belt and reached for my smokes.

"Easy now," a voice said. "Keep the hands where I can see them, Matlock." From over my left shoulder, coming out of nowhere.

I did as he said, didn't move, the voice somehow remembered, not threatening but hard.

"We met the other night," he said. "After they mopped the parking lot with your ass. Sara's my sister. I'm going to slide into the back seat. Be a good man and unlock the door."

I moved the hand slow and hit the button to spring the lock. I heard the door open and waited while he got settled. The door whispered 'click' and the part of my head that usually got whacked, behind the right ear and a little higher...that part started fidgeting, mousing up, expecting a rap. When nobody dropped in, I figured it was okay to talk. So I talked.

"The name's Maddock, Bear. You mind if I raise my arm? It's Bear, isn't it? Sara said her brother was called Bear." I raised my arm and felt the phantom knot on my head. The wonder of it all.

"I ain't got no gun, white man. Clumsy as you are I wouldn't need one. Sara says you're supposed to help. She sees far but I got my doubts. Gimme some history."

I rested my arm on top of the car seat and turned toward the back, just enough to look at my companion away in the dark there and big for sure but indistinct until one of the cars from the pumps wheeled out and around. I caught a flash of him then.

He was big all right with black ponytail hair the blue-sheen color of oil on captive water. He was wearing sunglasses at midnight, resting on a slightly broken nose. Hard shoulders that fell straight away to his waist. Barrel chest and an ass as flat as a mesa. Holding the white straw hat he took off to do his creepin'. Boots and a buckle and a wristwatch on one of those wide leather straps. A buckskin lace for a necklace with a single turquoise bead. In a sleeveless denim work shirt buttoned halfway up and a tattoo on his right shoulder that read something like 'Rangers'. Shit, he didn't need a gun.

"Gimme some more juice," I said. "It's under the passenger seat."

"You don't need no more. I could smell you before I could see you."

"Let me tell you somethin', Bear. It don't have no effect on me. Just makes me friendly."

"That right? You was certainly friendly last night."

"They slipped gamma hydrox in my drink, I fell hard."

"You're a piece of shit," Bear said and handed over the juice. He laughed. Some folks, they just go with the flow.

"Bear White Crow," I intoned and drained a slug. I wiped my lips with the back of the bottle hand and had another.

"Standing Bear, Maddock. You don't know Native, do you?"

"Big Daddy knew your people. It's why Sara trusts me. My Daddy's from there too."

"Sarah trusts you cause you been sent. By *Hashtahli*. Mystery to me but I'm just a humble servant. What's the plan, white eyes?"

"No plan yet. I got a friend on the way for back up is all. You two ought to get on real fine. Lavon's a freckle-assed, redheaded redneck. Used to be a little twisted but he's straightening out. That's my big army, Chief."

"You call me Chief again I'll snap your neck, Matlock. What say we try and get along."

"Works for me, Bear. Call me Maddock, okay? And I ain't exactly signed on...just studying the situation at this point. Deciding, you might say."

"You sent for your friend."

"I was mostly decided, only..."

"Only you're a yella piece of shit and don't like Native."

"I like Sara. I'm still deciding on you. Rangers is it? What do you need me for?"

"My plan was to go in there and gut the four of 'em. Sarah says that won't work so good. It's gotta come down different with this bunch - to make things stick. She says you're savvy, that you'll know how to handle these whites."

"Sara's got a lot of faith in me, man."

"It's not you, stupid. It's *Hashtahli*. You're just the tool."

"Maybe I'll walk, Bear."

"Ain't gonna happen, Matlock. Sara's seen it. She told me your fate is sealed. It's what gives you great power."

"Well, if everything is sealed, I guess I'll be heading back to the motel. Lavon arrives around noon, and I don't wanna keep the boy waiting. Besides, it's been a long day and I'll be needing my sleep."

I flicked the key to the ignition and the engine fired and I turned round to the back seat again. I was grinning like a coyote this time.

"Can I drop you somewhere, Bear?"

"I'm already home, Maddock. See you around twelve," he said and climbed from the car.

I watched as he headed off south, wearing his hat now and hugging the dark that circled the men's club. The ex-Ranger, wheeling his way through the Panhandle, parachute boots for moccasin. One more critter on the prowl and looking to dine.

Knocking down stars as he went.

WILLOUGHBY

It was all of four blocks across the overpass and down the frontage road to the Prairie View. I could have skipped a stone or just plain skipped it, but there I was once more, waist-deep in someone else's business, phantom knots growing on the old gourd. Like some long-defunct broken wheel, a discard from the Stone Age. Thick and dumb and out of round enough to make my life...interesting. Fifty-two cards and out falls a joker. Slipped in there to gum things up, start the kettle boiling. Everybody gettin' their fingers burned and my turn swinging by.

I went in through a lobby that was all aglow, 5 a.m. and the coffee fresh and the sweet rolls moist and shiny. Bulk cereal and bananas and apples, waiting for the first go-getter. The continental breakfast, free with the room. I grabbed an apple and polished it and headed for the second-floor landing. The deskman that didn't much care was staring, so I backtracked and gave him a smile. He had his palms together, a little church steeple.

"Hey, buddy. Nice morning," I said.

"They generally are, until the dogs start barking."

"Meaning?"

"Meaning, I get these feelings...not often but I got 'em now. You show up, check-in with three-day old welts. The next morning you got brand new ones on top of those. And this Injun the size of Godzilla drops you in a heap in the lobby - that Injun, by the way, is outside the motel every time I drive into the lot. Except he's like fog and I'm rubbing my eyes wondering. But that ain't enough so you hit on Dolores and turn the Wrangler upside down, the whole joint stoned, right down to Pepe, the dishwasher. I swear, somethin's goin' down. Just please give me a head start, fellah. I want to be long gone when it blows."

"Keep your skirt on, Shep," I told him reassuringly. "Nothing's gonna blow. The Native's an old army buddy. We're gonna have a reunion, soon as Lavon gets here. You'll know him by his red hair and kind of freckly skin. Wears a belt that says HOSS on the back. We all served," I said.

"I see, Mr. Maddock," the deskman said. Getting the name wrong, but who wasn't these days. His nose seemed to be growing too, getting a little sharper. Rat or fox was anybody's guess.

"Just Maddock," I said.

"As far as Dolores...I took a liking to her on account of her beauty and down-home, simple motives. A rare find in a woman these days. Wouldn't you say?"

"Don't know that I would," he said.

"I don't know no Pepe," I added.

"I see," he said again. "Then there's the call from a rather insistent Miss Evelyn...several calls in fact. I suppose she was a Marine, too," he said. His eyebrows were waving around like folks out of gas. Back in charge though, a spry little spinster with a .38.

"Ev was in the reserves. Artillery." I told him. "Now be a sport and send up some scrambled eggs, toast and bacon. Okay?"

"Not until six. Shall I throw on a 'tall and wet one'?" he inquired, a little snide but chummy.

"Sure. Tall and wet. I'd be much obliged," I said and bounded the staircase, three at a time.

I got to 209 and slipped the plastic card into the lock and listened. 'Click' the lock went and I shoved on in, home you might call it and I nearly did.

First thing I picked up the phone and started to dial Ev. Barely past four o'clock her time, but Ev was an early bird and I needed to know. Those repeated calls of hers could mean a couple of things, mostly bad. No one knew my phone number, my whereabouts, except Marie. So Ev called Marie to get a hold of me and Marie hadn't called me, so Ev hadn't put the fear in her. Or something like that.

I started to dial but replaced the phone and braided some nose hair. Maybe give it an hour or so on her end. Probably Ev was changing her ways, retired now and sleeping in. I gazed at the phone on the cradle and rocked on my heels. Something wrong with baby, but I wasn't listening.

I turned for the shower and off came the clothes, dropping them as I went, stepping lightly and looking forward to it. All the smoke and booze and Panhandle wind gone; Dolores' perfume and Standing Bear and his get-up...all of it, gone in the flood.

But in the stall, I'm thinking why not grease the sled, so out I pop, moving from the bath and making my way to the bedside table, dripping on the carpet as I go. I got ice from the bucket and fixed a drink on the rocks. Just a tip of the jug to all the gamers, to the brotherhood. Like a club tie or secret handshake between friends. A bridge between what was and what was coming. A habit I picked up along the trail, a trick I learned from a wise old duster.

'Take two drinks and call me in the morning' he used to say. 'Or don't.'

Well, it was morning and my fate was sealed, according to Sara Long Eyes, and that begged for something, a drink maybe, damned if I could recall. I was always a little short on imagination.

So back to the bath I trod, carrying my spoils and nearly made it too, ever so close until I slammed on the brakes and changed direction one more time. Next thing I'm reaching for the duffel shoved under the bed. I pulled out the nine-millimeter and took it with me, laid it on the sink just outside the shower. I covered it with a hand towel, like covering a spider.

It was that feeling you got sometimes. The one that made your stomach flip, kept you awake late. Maybe it was too early to be feeling that way. Maybe it wasn't. You didn't want to find out.

I plugged the gap beneath the door with the bathmat and opened the water full blast. I got the heat about right and stood there hangdog, exhausted beneath the falls, letting the steam build while affecting a slow and measured fade…like a twig, just floating away in the rain. Rolling and bobbing and spinning under and breaching that last time for air. I let the water take me all the way back, or nearly, and rode the salient points forward, the ones they hang your flesh on. Carried forward on a roaring flood of doubt.

It seemed a dream almost, this drifting on a river, but not quite, not so smooth or lucky - the mind a brace of high voltage lines buzzing in the silence, in the void, swaying in the emptiness. It went something like this the mind and its almost dream...somewhere a grandfather clock stands naked, bemused, alone amidst a storm of golden motes gently swirling, settling softly onto the minute hand, one upon the other, bending it down, piling on like so many coin. Time at a standstill under all that weight. Bent and barely room between the seconds, or flowing continuous somehow, a wave, a flurry of nothing...tired and broken old man time was, tall and stiff and wooden in his mahogany suit. Shiftless too, backed into the corner as he was and playing the dead man's hand. Tired, gaunt and riven the captive face, its gears gently clasping, gently turning away. Brass dentures softly milling time as the old guy swoons, the mouth goes slack, the corners anyway, falling ever so soundlessly. As heavy, leaden counterweights spiral down, sway suggestively, swirling in the backwash of time. While the pendulum, the golden scimitar, completes its arc. But no flesh and no bones. Just a rush of heat between the strokes. And all the while this whirring noise as though through space, as though time, the balance wheel tottering crazy. Yet one would never guess. One would never know.

Like death only kinder.

TREY AND THE DREAM

After the shower I canned the lights and pulled the curtains closed to make some dark, just as the sun was waking. I could have slept naked on Main Street in the middle of the Derby, I was that wasted. I lay with a towel for cover, my right arm under the bride's pillow, gripping the popgun. I didn't want anyone to get the jump on me, spoil the wedding. Me and my gat, holding hands like navy buddies, both of us loaded.

And I slept hard and fast, freewheeling that country where yes and no rehearse their lies. Wandering through the ether, no need for dirt with its furrows of patience. A vagrant mind, sawing at bones, longing to be done with them. A mind free, but for the body dangling, that nagging, forlorn body with all its hang-ups.

I lay that way for some time, motionless, anchored. The sleep coming deep and hard as I stumbled blind, blind until the light broke and the dream began...

All was shining in the dream, everything cherry, the skates were golden. In a world of constructs, I wasn't drunk, cornered, dead or buried. I wasn't being pursued, no one wanted my neck. If anything, I was the pursuer and I was bounding. I was chasing a golden beam from a golden vault. All my old friends were there.

Fear and guilt, pain and worry, those other saddle tramps I broke trail with, rode along with the recent months, in my dream they were gone. Tumbled into the gorge and so be it. Companions but never friends, wiped clean like tin soldiers, melted in the deep slumber, vanished along with their toy souls.

And clean were the hands and what lightness to the eyes in the images rushing forth as from a childhood long since buried. A moment's perfection amongst all that buried time. As when the heart first opens, real warm and peaceful, a sunny bower in an azure forest of spruce and pine. Splendid was the world with its arcing light, green and brown verdant earth, water the color of a prism, sparkling crystal waves.

In the dream there was Charlie, my old buddy Charlie, dead before his time. I didn't suppose I would ever be rid of Charlie, and that was good. Funny how someone dead and gone can be your rock. The whole of one's passage anchored fast in the wake of remembering.

And there was Salome also, the woman I bawled to Sara about. A spirit by the time I met her, and that just a maybe, all the faith I could muster.

All of them ghosts now, calling me to the reunion. Crazy, I guess. It's what happens when you take a gun in your hands. It's what you mortgage, the last tie you sever when you walk that path, stumble onto a world of commandments. Part of you dead, but not enough or not yet woken and ain't that a shame.

There came the flashes of different places also, and the moods and fragrances associated with other, further times. The music of memory and muscles twitching like dog running down rabbit in its dream. Vibrating like a harp.

One moment youthful, the very next I was older, a wise old gray head. And even in the dream I knew that was a long shot, the doddering old tot would not likely be. Even there it was not in the cards, and I became young again quickly, almost at once in a dream stumbling ever forward, and that not often a sign of longevity. Say goodbye to the long view back it seemed to be saying. But in the dream, I let that one go, not a second thought, as the leaf flutters onto a stream and is gone. Something else was urging me on.

And then I was splashing into the second river, riding a mare with a flash of white on her forehead, busted across and now I knew that it was the second river and there was left but one stretch more of ground to cover. A long and tenuous stretch. One more stretch until you came to the third river and beyond, the last you would ever cross.

Call it an almost life. You needn't look hard for it. The last river and one fine morning you arrive. Or sleep takes you over, the unfinished thoughts, the ones you'll die with tumbling one onto the other.

Which darkened things a bit, some of the light fell out of the dream about then and the other world came clambering back, hungry for its fair share. Waking me from my peace. Rapping at my soul, an echo in the vaulted forest…except it was only room service, 6:05 a.m. and the deskman that didn't much care was good as his word. A Denver omelet for the desperado from up North…and a tall and wet one, compliments of the house - though I was waterlogged and needn't be topped. But I could always chug it later. I always had.

The young man who rolled it in was named Trey, a sharp kid from town or one of the farms or ranches thereabouts. Scraping some dough for college or a pickup or just to keep his taw. He was all business, wheeling the food around and removing the covers with a practiced flair. He turned the cup over and poured the coffee, set the plates and silver, everything just so. And all the while he was talking in this pleasant, soft voice. He was talking low, fluttering those young boy lashes as he served. He was making a pitch.

"A guy today has gotta hustle to get ahead. Yes sir, work faster and longer is my motto. That's why I like the service work, the hospitality business. I can get a guy anything...I take pride in it. Make their stay a little more comfortable, if you know what I mean. Whatever they want, they all ask for Trey."

Trey looked at me in a sly sort of way. Pointing at me with thin nostrils that give a pinched look, fighting for air. Little sticks of dynamite for eyes. Not too polished at the grift yet, but young still, a sparkler. Throw the kid a bone, he might be a comer.

"Tell you what Trey," I said and dangled a twenty. "Get the desk to hold all my calls, would'ya, until eleven and then buzz me. Have a ham sandwich and coke delivered at a quarter after. Can you handle it? Can you keep the world at bay?"

"Consider it done, Mr. Maddock. Like I mentioned, a guy's gotta hustle," he said. "You want the fries with that?" he asked, and I nodded, keeping it simple. And just like the wind, Trey and his cart were gone, down the hall and out of earshot.

What I bought with my twenty was silence, about as cheap as you'll ever pay, and I was mighty high on myself. High enough I got ready to dine. I slid the gun from under the covers and into the drawer, on top of the Gideon, and sat at the canasta table and unfolded my napkin and placed it on my lap. Something wrong though and this light was flickering, so I took the gun back out of the drawer and placed it on the chair next to the table. I looked at it laying there but it never said a word. Not a peep. The Good Book too had long since spoken.

I closed the drawer then and surveyed my castle keep, looking for friends or anybody, any kind of company, while I gnawed on the omelet. In between I swilled hot java and whistled show tunes, mostly. Tight with the world is what I'm saying. Tired for certain, but a couple hours sleep and I'd have my edge back.

On top of that I now had all the angles. Found them in the breeze. The steam from the shower, the aborted nap had made me wise, and it was all coming back. Sometimes you gotta forget to remember and I thought on that for a while, went through the list and it wasn't a long one: Didn't need a smoke or a drink. Didn't even need a plan. Good thing, too. One for deuce is all the house allows. So, I did the next best thing. I passed on go and gave my lover Daphne a call. I gave a call to the call girl and when she didn't answer I left a message, a short but sweet one: "Calling all angels..." it began, all sugar and roses - but Dolores and I had always been about business. So I finished the message off with a lie.

And then I pulled the curtain down.

TREY

It was ten thirty when I woke, my mind finally clear of all the fluff and dreams and carousel ponies. Those little island words, the poetry of it all, channeled round comma's set adrift by the mind. The royal mind and its court of fools.

I woke sober and that was maybe a highlight. Clear and sharp as canyon ice, unmolested by man, but only just. With a crisp, distant ticking sound that I took a liking to. A metronome...for what kind of music? You tell me. That was the part I never could fathom, the conduit and wires and sheet metal and solder. I never could break through, not like with the fleshy part, the blood and brains and the grand emotions. I knew the flesh all right, with its heat and its pain. I was a big thinker that way. Except the spark. I never could figure where the spark came from. Soul or machine? But in the end, just another faithless sod.

So, it was off into a blind future and I was blind and I guess that meant I was ready. The old story of the three rivers everyone has to cross, just a memory now and no way out of that one. I let it go and figured to meet up with it again sometime. Out there in the mist with the long gone and not so very long gone, at the river's edge, shoving off from the bank. I never thought it was going to be easy, letting go and it never was. But sometimes you gotta toss the bodies if you want to get airborne and I went with that, the mind did anyway.

I took a quick shave and made coffee in the room. I powdered up and dressed in a hurry too while prowling my campsite. First, I counted my store of medicine, everything in order. Next, I shoved the twenty-two bundles of dough into the duffel bag, one of them light, the three thousand I'd wired to Lavon. Marie had another twenty and Lavon's ex had four and Lavon had one. Then there was the fifty I'd deposited into the bank a little bit at a time, thinking I might want to pull cash with plastic while on the run. Lighting up the map like a pachinko parlor and leaving a nice trail. Sending up flares in case I got lost or someone wanted to put a trace on me. Forgetting about the two hundred thousand flappin' around in the trunk of my car. And all the rest of it, scattered like birdseed from here to Denver. Three hundred thousand. Don't go as far as it used to.

I lit a smoke and moved to the window and cracked it wide. Ten-thirty and starting to warm, but still that humidity from the night before. I always liked to walk in it, return home fresh and wakeful. But that was some time ago and I had long since lost the happy-go-luckys. The message I was getting now was garbled and haywire but clear nonetheless. A palm reader could see it a mile away. No lifeline, amigo.

So, I crossed the room and fished for the amber colored stuff in the flask. I took a pull and tossed it back into the sack. It was all about business now, I wasn't cavorting. I checked the nine-millimeter and dropped the clip and counted seven. The Wingmaster lay under the bed and I brought it out and checked the magazine and the safety mechanism. It had gone from the backseat to the trunk of my car to the closet during the night. I wanted it warm and the gun slick running for Lavon. It might raise a few eyebrows, but it was totally legal and nasty and you wanted it nasty. A good friend to have at the party.

Next, I called Ev. I hadn't forgotten her, just misplaced her in the rush. I got the answering machine and her standard message had been changed. Now her voice announced: "If you want to reach Evelyn...all you gotta do is whistle."

I listened to the dead air and when the tone sounded, I hung up and stood there rocking on my heels, trying to shake that sinking feeling. The whistle business was a signal we invented in case Ev ever needed to clear out. Twenty years we never had to use it. Until now. All my karma a whirlpool, sucking the whole crowd down.

I grabbed the attaché off the canasta table and got out the little address book with all the little addresses. I flipped through and found the number for Evelyn's sister Dolly. I thought about a trace on the line, the chances, the likelihood of it all caving in. But I'd already dialed Ev, so if anyone was fishing, I was good as cooked. Strange world. Every step a footprint leading back to your lair. Keep you home Friday nights, if you let it.

So I reached for the phone and it rings mid-air but I didn't jump, flinch or shout. I was bloodless as marble now, no pulse. Just a wink from my twin at the shadow's edge of memory. My double from the jungles of hell. Zoned out, locked and loaded. He told me he had my back as I lifted the receiver. Everything was cool.

"Maddock," I said.

"It's one minute 'til eleven, Mr. Maddock," Trey said.

"Morning again, Trey," I replied, shifting into something comfortable.

"Yes sir, it is. There's a hot pot of coffee outside your door. Compliments. The sandwich will be there at quarter after, like we planned. In the meantime, sir, I've got these people hid all over and around the motel and I need your permission to bring them up."

"What sort of people, Trey?" I asked.

"Well, there's Dolores, sir, and this sort of milky white, freckly fella. Bright red comb like a rooster. His belt says 'HOSS'. I got them stashed in the Wrangler. And there's another one that's sort of mobile," he said. He said 'bile' as in mile.

"He's a slick one, ain't he Trey?"

"Yes sir. Quick like a bantamweight only he must go two-twenty easy."

"That would be Bear."

"Yes sir. Bear. We got an arrangement already. I been gettin' him food and he's been showing me tricks."

"You're coming along fast, Trey."

"Not enough hours in the day, sir," he said.

"We may need to find a few more then. Tell you what, Trey, I just slipped a hundred-dollar bill under the lamp sitting here on the bedside table. You earned it. You with me Trey?" I asked.

"Yes sir," he said.

"I like the way you handle things, Trey, so I'm putting another hundred under there with the first. You might be able to help me."

"The whole business is hospitality, Mr. Maddock. It's sort of my motto," Trey replied. I could hear him breathing fast and shallow now, doing the math.

"I want you to send everyone up to the room in about ten minutes. Bring a party tray along when you deliver my sandwich, enough for the whole crowd. Throw some cokes along with it. After we've had our lunch, I'll get back to you concerning that second hundred. I may need an operative in the Panhandle."

"I knew you were somebody," Trey said. "I just knew it."

"But can you keep a secret?" I asked him.

"Ask me no secrets, I'll tell you no lies," he whispered as the phone got heavy and the line went dead.

EVELYN AND THE DOLLY LAMA

I replaced the phone and looked around the motel room and buddy, there's no place like home. I lifted the receiver again and dialed the Dolly Lama, Ev's sister, what she called her when they were disagreeing, which was most of the time. Ev being kind of a freewheeler while Dolly was tight as a corset.

Dolly picked up and I told her it was Maddock and she tossed me over to Evelyn fast, like bath water out the window. Dolly had gotten over my kind of soft shoe long before I met her, which was a good thing.

I listened to the pause while Ev covered the mouthpiece and told Dolly to beat it, the call was private, and then she was on the line.

"Maddock," she said.

"Hang on, Ev," I told her and lay the phone on the bedspread. I unzipped the duffel and fished for and found the scotch flask but shoved it aside for the clear stuff. I didn't want badger breath with company so near and dear. I screwed the jar to my lips and gave it a practiced flip of the wrist.

"I'm back darling. What's this about blowing in your ear?" I asked.

"Just whistle, Maddock. The signal was 'just whistle'. And don't call me darling. Remember the signal? You probably can't see the smoke from where you are but believe me, the barns on fire. You said if things ever got hot...well, the bacon's sizzling."

"Give me a hint Ev. Twenty five words or less."

"Stanley White got conked on the head, but he's going to make out. Stitches and bruises, but it might have been worse. They tossed his office - your old office - but they got the wrong guy. Guess who they were looking for?" she asked.

I hung there quiet and still, sort of dangling in front of her question, staring it square in the eye. All the while I'm contemplating another belt. 'Hell to you, world' was pretty much what I was thinking.

"Maybe he got wise with the cable guys," I told her finally and took the drink fast, as planned, but not like a virgin this time. I took it with a purpose.

"Maybe so," Ev replied, "only next it's my turn and I get a couple of heavy breathers on the phone and some dark sedans trolling the neighborhood until it looked like they were coming my way. So I got out fast. I'm staying with Whoosit until you give me a 'coast is clear.'"

I shook my head but it was empty. This might be one of those times where the coast never clears.

"This might be one of those times when the coast never clears, Ev," I told her.

"Oh jolly, I was hoping you were going to say that. So I sell my house and join you on the...what do we call it these days? The lam?" she asked. Eleven a.m. and I could hear the blush chardonnay talking. I thought about another myself.

"By now they already got whatever it is you could give them, Ev. I don't think it reaches any farther on your side. We sit tight. You stay where you are. If you need money, you're still a signer on the business account. Go to the bank, it's got thirty or so. Just watch your back. Also, I'm not on the lam, I'm exercising my prerogatives."

"About those prerogatives. What do we tell her?"

"We'll tell Marie to get one giant step removed. When it looks like the coast has cleared, I'll have you give her a call. Or vice versa. Be circumspect while you're on the telephone Evelyn and don't forget to write. Oh, and thanks for the memories," I purred, laying a soft one in on her ribs.

"De nada, Maddock," she whispered. "De nada, de nada" she whispered again as a silence settled on the line and the phone went dead.

CUT THE CARDS

So that's what a sixteen-footer looks like all dashed on the rocks, splinters everywhere and a bunch of moaners washed up on the beach. Bait and tackle and beer and the baby's ass all hung out everywhere. Bobbing in the drink. So that's what it looks like I told myself.

"Might want to get it right from here on out," I mentioned sort of casually. "You never were much of a swimmer," I hastened to add but I wasn't laughing, just a pool room smirk for all the gawkers. All none of them.

Which left maybe ten minutes of solitary before the bomb squad arrived: Lavon, Daphne and the Bear. Oh, and Trey, I was definitely going to be needing Trey now that Plan Z was all but fleshed out. Plan Z, whatever you want to call it, don't never you worry, it can't miss. It's the old 'last house on the left' plan. It's always the last house on the left. Only don't even knock, just tumble on in. Everybody's waiting.

Sitting above the fracas you'll find Sara White Crow, above all us poor mortals apparently, pounding on her tom-toms. And above her is *Hashtahli*, pulling the strings. I'm playing base fiddle in an all-brass band, third chair and last, until poof! - I been promoted. Whatever was going down before has just got serious.

The trouble with Ev and White, the tossing of my old office, Lavon and his girl and their heartache, all of it reached me with an accumulated force I had to reckon with. I would have bet a hundred to one the bad guys wouldn't corner me in ten years. If you'd asked, that is. And while I'm betting, I'm thinking, 'Probably never'. Instead, a couple days is all it takes to get warm and now they're getting warmer. Leaving me no time for the big swoon, the denial. And way too late to bail.

So back I head to the sack, for one last look at the money or the gun or for a snoot full or just a reminder before I drop myself in and zip it shut. A reflex was all. To help the dumbster get his bearings. Like the porch light glowing at the end of Shady Lane and pretty simple really. It nearly always is once you blow the smoke away.

I put the shotgun back beneath the bed and shoved the duffel under there with it. Then I thought better of that and pulled the thin bundle out of the bag and riffed it. Seven thousand was plenty motivation, enough for Daph and the kid I figured, with some left over. No sense confusing things, just give 'em some money. I put the wad in my pocket.

Then I flitted around the room a while longer and plumped pillows and opened shades. A high-noon Panhandle wind was blowing hot, leaving a little drift of sand on the ledge where the window lay open a crack. Some kind of reminder if you were one for hints, played that sort of game. Time chasing its tail and all of that, but I was blind to it, rushing as I was, neck and neck with the dark.

Straight across the interstate Gentleman Jim's was sparkling but I didn't take notice of that either, just listened to the high whine of a semi sailing by. I floated over to the sofa and found my place and sort of nestled above the cushions. Killing time and more than enough of that, so I went back to work on the big plan, fleshed it out some more in my head. Hoping against hope I'd done my homework all those years. Practiced up on the three d's: drinking, ducking and dying. And all the while I'm thinking there are certain disasters to which there is no recourse.

Lightning comes to mind. The La Brea tar pits, another favorite. What they used to call a tough break before the big bad world went all sour inside. On and on I went, feeding an ice cream headache with another scoop of the Rocky Road. Blathering, and all of it tumbling around inside my gourd, out of line and topsy-turvy. So that I put a stop to it, I gave myself an order.

"Shut the fuck up, Maddock," I told myself as a knock came on the door and I was saved, I swear I was. 'Arbeit Macht Frei' the knuckles rapped as I headed off to greet the gang. Stopping only to grab the auto and slip it into the back of my waistband.

Recalling as always what Daddy used to say - 'Trust everybody...but cut the cards...'

THE MEET

It was Dolores and Lavon knocking at the door, standing in the hallway and looking like a couple of evangelists got the day all wrong and their directions crossed, clear out of bounds and wandering blind down the dark end of nowhere. Or the welcome wagon. One wheel in the ditch and the pot roast on the lawn. But a kind of peacefulness for all that. Lavon was grinning.

"Hey Lavon," I said and moved aside to allow them to enter. "Long time no loco."

"You can say that again," Lavon replied, waiting for Dolores to step inside. "I guess you and Dolores have met," he says and aims her gently through the doorway. "Otherwise, I'm in the wrong movie."

"It's your movie, alright. Hello, Dolores," I said. "Thanks for going to get Lavon."

"The pleasure was mine," she says. She stands there vibrating, fresh and yellow as corn cakes.

"I rented a car like you told me, got a Ford though, a white Mustang convertible, but I left the top up. I didn't want his shock of red hair to start a stampede." She laughed and nudged Lavon and he began smiling too. He had that crazy red color hair and skin white as lunch bread and you could see his color rising.

"What with the message you left me, I just had to see what this guy looked like," she said.

"Come again?" says Lavon. They had not come unstuck from her nudge and he was still smiling and friendly and leaning against her. There was an inquisitive cast to his face though as he looked from Dolores to me.

"Maddock told me to pick a guy up at the bus station. Said he looks like a saltlick with a cherry on top." She said this while gazing at Lavon and he was gazing at her and their eyes were locked and he was grinning now.

"Least I got one," he said, and they whinnied like donkeys, eyes for each other alone. I'm standing to the side wondering when I'm supposed to jump in, like it's still my show.

"Did I miss something?" I asked. "You two long lost twins or what?"

Lavon looks at her and there's a pause and Dolores starts in. Both twitching like chipmunks now.

"As best we can tell its chemical," Dolores says. "Instant."

"Love at first sight," Lavon chimes in and my mind is sailing off, over the Interstate. Where was I when they changed the channel? Nevertheless, I swallow it down quick and look at my watch. Time hasn't stopped moving, just had some fun while I wasn't looking.

"I'm glad we cleared that up. Y'all still in?" I ask and Lavon is already rocking his head, smiling yeah. Dolores smiles too. The lotus at the toe of Buddha smiles. The whole world is smiling. I don't say a word, I'm waiting for the axe to fall but Dolores wants to keep on talking.

"Lavon told me some things about you. You're no cowboy at all," she says. "You're a kidder is what you are."

"Did Lavon tell you how we met?" I ask her and glance over at Lavon studying the ceiling.

"Not exactly. Only that you hit it off."

"Oh yeah. He hit it off first and I hit it off second. Now we're one big happy family. You're family too, Dolores,"

"That makes me warm all over. You fellas burn down Gentleman Jim's and take Harley Reece down with it and I'll melt in your mouth, not in your hands." She says this straight to my eyes and my cheeks probably dapple some, but I don't blink. She's got her motor running, cranking out about 4000 rpm's. Just keeping things well-oiled now that she's almost married.

"So anyway, Lavon says you got business to tend to and then he's mine. You can drop him off after work?"

"Absolutely. I'll have Trey drop him off," I say. "In a couple hours." I peel three thousand off the roll in my pocket and hand it over.

"I may need a few more favors," I tell her.

"Oh, I'll be around, Maddock," she says and shoves it into her purse. Then she gives Lavon a peck on the cheek and it's quick for the door. Lavon opens it wide and out she flies while his head rolls round the jamb, holding on tight.

I catch a quick draft of air as Lavon turns back to the room. Fishing in my pocket, palming the four thousand I promised him and like that I'm empty. Forgot all about Lavon's four and now the whole wad is shot. The stuff just flies less you're sitting on it. I glance over at Lavon.

"That's quite a woman," I tell him.

"Oh yeah, she's a keeper for sure," Lavon says while studying the hand in my pocket. "All these good things happening to me, coming to me from the wrong way and the wrong side. And now you give me a job and benefits too. I'm the luckiest guy in the world."

"Right you are," I tell him and throw the shotgun on the duvet. "Your luck just keeps on coming. You ever seen one of these?" I ask.

"Plenty. So tell me about this job. See if I guessed right. We gonna knock off the four o'clock stage?"

"Something like that, Lavon," I says. "You been drinking?" I ask.

"Should I be?" Lavon says, starting to grin.

"Time will tell," I tell him. You had to admire a guy like Lavon, walking cold sober into a box canyon. Shit for brains maybe, but tough as cat gut. And always faithful.

"In the meantime, why don't we wash up. I got food from room service on the way and our third man should be here soon so we can all rehearse our lines. That is, if you're still feeling lucky."

That's when I pitch him the four thousand he's due, wound tight as a lie though not nearly so heavy. Up it goes and down it twirls and he catches it soft and easy. Rolling it in his palm, weighing it the way you measure the quiet before that first scream, when all the shooting starts. That cold, dead, hollow quiet.

"Lucky?" Lavon inquires, his eyes drilling into mine. "Not really… just wondering if we're the good guys this time."

"Will it break your heart if I tell you," I says, and Lavon is shaking his head side to side. He's sighting down the barrel.

"It's loaded with double aught. Put a hole in a Frigidaire. But we don't wanna use it," I tell him. "Just carry it for looks."

"I'll have that drink now," he says and drops the shotgun on the bed. I fish the red stuff out and pour him a real one. I grab mine and we clank jars and Lavon makes the first toast:

"Here's to Dolores," Lavon says. "The woman I love."

"And here's to Sara White Crow and Leah, the little Autumn Dove," I tell him as we run 'em down fast.

Out on the Interstate a trucker blows his horn, two dots and a dash, while from the near side comes a knocking on the door. Some kind of message if you care to play that game, connect those kinds of dots. A signal. Like the smoke from a distant mesa, or the murmur rising from a dense, darkening wood. Or that mourning song the breezes play on a vast, impersonal prairie. A sign that all is as it ever shall be, as it ever was. Heaven above and hell below and in between this thin, tenuous middle ground.

I glance at Lavon and recognize the dream, come out of myself, has found its other.

"Time to feather up, Lavon" I tell him. "Time to paint your pony."

THE LANDING

Three a.m. on the highway south, a glide plane to Lubbock. It's always 3 a.m. somewhere. They just give it a different hour.

The world is thin at this remove, all tumble down to the ocean, a cascade through the hard, ample shoulders that ride the top of middle Texas. But thin on the eastern flank, the horizon, like a closed eye in repose. Waiting on the light.

You come in for a landing at night, the amateur pilot and his whiz-kid gyroscope, the old pilot's watch ablaze with dots of radium. Tattered cloth from the glider's wing rips the silence, tears it asunder the way a wayward heart is torn. Except it is only highway now, wide and empty and vacant of the impatient summer crowds, the vacationers still tucked within their bungalow dreams. But the truckers flow on, all restless, relentless, moving fast and gray in the night.

"South, we're heading south," you say but do not hear. Only the car's motor and then sometimes the wind.

Highway whispers past, the tearing sound of nylon on a big girl's thigh. Her floral print summers dress diaphanous, floating on an orange breeze. You hold the road and hover above the little honeybee, above the moist heat rising, mere inches from pay dirt. There you are in your mind, a poet, floating, and you've found yourself at last, lost though you were for a moment in her eyes. That precious moment with nature's root bestirring. Plant your flag, dreamer.

"You're a poet Maddock, only nobody cares."

'Screw thyself,' the poet replies still managing the road.

"One line at a time," I affirm while staring into fields sown heavy with darkness. Away in the distance the chicken coops with their solitary lights aglow and their little chicken hearts beating row upon row and the nest lights glowing on glowing off. Shining down like a curse. Sheds and pump houses and silos and barn doors - all tin-sided and clasped shut and hollow. Farther off but closing fast comes the coyote, warily testing the wind, while grandma and grandpa hold down the wedding bed. A solitary shotgun bears witness in the corner.

A crowd of headlights rush from the caravan of trucks urging us on from behind. To the fore a string of red eyes running warm, strung along the ridges of dark. A handful of trucks on the move, boxed and glowing in the amber outline of their trailers. The San Antonio, Austin, Corpus loads and all the side hauls to boot. Jacked-up and highballing. Liking the wide-open road, the white line, but praying for sunrise. Pulling into Corpus Christi, that first light Anno Domini. Now there's a rush. Blue ocean the color of sky. Sand the color of bone burning crosswise on the shore. But no pyre, not on this morning.

This morning flags as on a parapet, softly pulsing in the lift of a rising day. There will always be one you tell yourself. Always a new morning, the first day thereafter, with sinners clogging the beaches, the sons and daughters in procession, wading out to yet another eternity. One more lasting pity.

I light a smoke, no longer look inward for the message. Where would I find it? In dazzled eyes wavering behind the glow? What to look for, anyway. I don't need no grief. I bought my share already.

All of it, the whole hideous share. Bought it in ignorance, pride. I'll bury it there too, in the booze or the last lying moment. No witness to the waves curling over sailor boy, the glistening bubbles chasing his pale body down. No ashes this time, no dust. As if dust would matter. And likewise, no tears.

"You could always go out in a hail of bullets," I remind myself. Yes. But the game is hide and seek now, the old game and well you know it.

'You can't win by winning,' the mind posits. The restless mind, spiraling down.

"How so?" asks the dead man's eyes, sharing his fear with the rearview mirror.

'You only lose by losing,' the thinker responds.

"Yes? Good."

I run the dial on the AM. Nothing but static and the whistling, disturbing tone of radio chaos as we roll through hardpan and onto the flats that pour south from the Panhandle. A different lay to the land and a culture that speaks to permanence. Where the steeple bell's song reaches those only who wish to be had. Dust and sweat and the noonday sun for clothes.

I make the lights of town in that almost blue of morning, the exit sign guiding me in with open arms. The hotel bed, cold and chaste, receives me while through the window a timorous arc of light licks the eastern edge. A spinster's blush, beckoning as I run the curtains cross, closing off the scene. Nighttime and its dubious cloak benign.

Gone.

THE BIG KNOCK-OVER

We blew a hole in the sky all right, clear through to Kingdom Come and then some, with everybody flying willy-nilly, plummeting down quick in that dark and landing on the run. The whole gang, like shooting stars, flaming out over the Panhandle. Two a.m. and the big wide world just a nasty little affair that was getting nastier fast. Everything awful and mean and close and tight and then it just blew. The six of us in the back room of Gentleman Jim's, and that was five too many. Tossed me halfway to Lubbock before I got my bearings. Shook me right out of my reverie so that I pulled up short and jumped the exit into Plainview.

Funny end to it too. For something that started out calm enough and almost lyrical, for just another low-key early morning hour's stick-up, it sure took an ugly turn. You read about 'em all the time. But you had to be there for this one, front row center. Lavon and his newfound love of theater:

"Jerkwater Jane's!" he yelled while swinging the sawed-off at the room of them and butt whacking the distinguished, older, silver-haired gentleman that called him a punk. Tipping him over. The old guy going "Ga-ah," as he cartwheeled behind the desk. And just like that we were standing inside.

"Pop goes the weasel!" Lavon hollered as he caught him on the chin and neck with the gunstock whipping through. Not pretty and I'll say that for it, everybody wound plenty tight and the clock halfway stopped it appeared and no shadow anywhere as the slick oldtimer hit the floor. He landed like a mess of hairpins: legs tangled, arms bent funny and shooting off in all the wrong directions. He lay there in a very sharp, very gay glen plaid that was looking a little ruffled now. Wide lapels and a medium blue stripe with matching vest to hide his old guy paunch. Topped off with a broad silk tie of maroon, gray and black regimental stripes, strewn on a pewter field. And a silver tie clip, twinkling gaily. Very rich and blended just so with his silver hair and flinty eyes. The tie laying twisted some, belly up now like the old guy. But that didn't seem to matter either.

The platinum-frame glasses he was wearing had skittered off beneath the desk and come to rest where I could see them lying next to his black, handmade Italian pumps. Shined to a patent leather sheen. He'd come sliding into home, a runner bringing it from third. But he never made it; he was out by a mile.

"You're out," Lavon said and came around fast on the other guys and racked the slide and out popped an unspent shell spinning lazy where it landed on the dark, mahogany desk. Round and round on the big shot's desk.

"There's three more in the tube in case you're wondering," Lavon hollered. He was wearing a black wool cap, full face with slits for eyes and mouth and nose. There was a trace of red hair poking from one of the eye slots and he kept working at it, winking at it, trying to clear his vision. It made him look like he was joshing when he told everybody to freeze, the eyelid flapping like a window shade. It made him look awful risky.

"Somebody's goin' down," he croaked with a voice that kept rising, higher even than the barrel he waved at the three of them, squirming now they got the picture, their faces run dry and tight as plaster with all that blood draining away at their feet.

It was long past time to swallow, but none of us in that bunch remembering exactly how, just rabbits in the road, wrinkling them noses, fixed by the headlights coming on. He got everybody's attention in a hurry and made me just a tiny bit jumpy myself. Why I paid him the big bucks, I guess. He was a sight.

"You can count on it. First one who moves... blooey!" Lavon hollers and that was my cue. First though I take in his heroic style, the jawbone swinging out. And that one eyelid still flappin' like a flag. A couple of hacks, headliners at the county work farm - Earl and Merle, the roommates. But enough of that and I take my cue.

"So nobody moves," I barked, only louder, and nobody did. Shame too, would have made things easier if one of them had high tailed for the prairie...

Instead, nobody moved as a ruckus began outside and the door burst open and there was the Bear. You think Lavon looked scary with that mask and sawed-off, you should have caught a glimpse of Bear. He had a blade for skinning in his mitt and a purple, mottled complexion that was straining hard behind mirrored shades. Like he was holding everything in. He looked like death on a war party. He looked like the end of the world.

Seems that little Leah was gone, vanished from the hooch they'd cobbled together for some of the girls, the starlets, off the backside of the strip club. And Leah was the main attraction. The big star. Why we was there. Only now it seemed she was vamonos!, gone south with Sonny, punk spawn of Harley Reece. Bear's little girl had flown.

Getting interesting I'm thinking but no time now with Bear on the move, grabbing the closest one, the taller of the three and banging him with the knuckle-side of the knife. Down he goes. I look at the other two and sort of slide to the end of the line.

"Gut 'em, Bear," Lavon yelps and now he's beginning to drool. That one red eyelid is fluttering fast, like a hummingbird, like somebody riffing cards and he's huffing sharp whistling breaths through the mask. Little pearls of spittle are starting to dangle, caught up in the wool of the mouth hole, swaying there in the mist.

"Murder one, pardner," I remind him. "We stick with the plan."

Whereupon Lavon drags out his pointed look and tries the fit for a quick half second until he's straight again and tall and right away I know he's snapped out of it. He's got his eyes locked forward.

"Right you are," he says and the both of us watch the Bear to see what's up, but Bear has gone savvy. Just flicks his chrome lenses to let us know we're on the same page.

"Phew!" Lavon says and glances my way. All I can muster, a dry little whistle, hops out and skitters along the wall.

Somewhere in that mix I piped Bad Eyes on the head with the automatic while Lavon and Bear tied up the messenger. And all the while I'm going for the hard drive and found it easy and folded the laptop and looked for the cash box and found it easy too. They weren't expecting to be strong-armed on account they knew who the bad guys were and they was it. And now they were beat and light about seven thousand by my reckoning and I handed it to Bear and gave Lavon the old 'let's get out of here' and then we were gone. For virgins it went by awful fast and pain free and slick as a brass monkey. Over before you got started maybe and not much to hold on to, but mighty interesting while it lasted. Just no future in it, the robbery business.

So we headed out through the back hall that made a dressing room for the big, grand show palace and a couple of the showgirls were still hanging out and one of them said "Hey, take me with you," and she wasn't kidding but Lavon said "Get your own horse," and then we were gone.

HASTA LA VISTA

After I tossed Sara, Bear and the tom-toms into the backseat of the Ford and shut the door on them and Lavon and Daphne but no Leah; and after Lavon did his rooster tail for show in the gravel back where they'd stashed the car - looking for all the world like a circus act while waving his arms and flappin' his wings; after all that I beat it back to the Prairie View motel and upstairs quick to room 209, straight as an arrow. Well, mostly straight but not quite.

The deskman who didn't much care appeared and put the stop on me in the lobby. He was growing fond of me it turns out.

"You're priceless," he said. "The hours you keep, the company. We haven't seen a show like yours in a month of Sundays."

"I swallow swords, too," I said, and the deskman fluttered a bit, a slight pitter-patter of the heart before he regained his composure. Found his grip in a hurry.

"Honestly, Maddock, it's been a pleasure. Any last requests?" he asked. He was standing stock still at 4 a.m. Clean, pressed and at your service. He was wearing that mortuary smile. His hand was out.

"Tell you what, Willoughby. If anybody asks, tell them you don't remember," I said and grabbed his paw.

"I can do that," he says, and we shake hands. Buddies after all.

I continue methodically on, up the stairs to 209, inching my way into the darkness night had made of my room. Lights off, everything vacant and hollow. Somebody's echo hiding somewhere in some corner, waiting for something to happen. A lot of some's for so young a morning but none of them in that crowd making much sense. A trail I tramped often now that Charlie made bail, but I wasn't going down that road no more.

Instead, I shoved the curtains aside and propped my elbows on the window ledge and stared over at the truck stop. Bright at that distance, never sleeping. The coffee shop glowing in that amber haze but the junk shop dead and glazed over and nobody at the pumps. Not a soul.

I ran my eyes down to Gentleman Jim's where a sedan had turned on its headlights and watched as another set of headlights popped on. The pair of automobiles found reverse and backed out in tandem, wheeling round and driving away together. The whole gang limping home after a night to remember. I guess the crime game got turned up a notch for the boys. Wrapping your lips round a scattergun will make most evenings memorable. That Lavon. What a trip.

I suppose Count Bueno, the old gray fox had a welt the size of an apple on his jaw. Dealing in drugs and skin, look what it got him. A made lieutenant, garrisoned in Amarillo. Still, he was family.

The one that messed me up the night before, the dangerous one, got piped on the head with the barrel of my nine-millimeter. He went down in a hurry and didn't come up. I wanted to kick him where he lay, in the groin or throat but no decent way to do it, so the feeling passed. Until a big wave of nostalgia for all the whippings I'd been getting crashed over me, remembering Enrique and the lashing little dance he did on my face. So I lay one in on the down guy's ribs.

The third one we tied with lamp cord, and he thought he was going to die. I gave him the message for Reece and that was all we made of the affair, the whole thing blown with Leah gone, down in Corpus with the big shot owner and his son now, and Bear fixing to torch the block and a half settlement, all the way to the gas pumps when Lavon hollers at him:

"Come on Bear, let's skedaddle," and the two of them piling in with the girls as I shut the car door. Leaning in I remarked to the assembled, "Don't you worry about Leah. And don't forget to write."

Closing the door, I stared in at Sara White Crow and caught her eye and for that moment our hearts held and there was a promise. It was all a circle and Sara's and mine had crossed and joined and we knew that and there was comfort in that for her at least.

Me? I gave up on comfort, except the Southern kind, and maybe with Marie one more time but maybe not. Time would tell but time was its own boss and bosses and me, well I never much cared. So I beat it back to the Prairie View, room 209.

The car was packed, the room paid up and nothing much big going on. I laid the room card on the chest of drawers and pulled the door shut on a patch of light lying square on the carpet. All that dark and still the light had seeped its way in. It lay there captive now, pulsing.

I slipped out of the room and went down the long hall to the exit off the far end of the motel and climbed into my car and I started her up. Then we sat a spell in the dirt idling, waiting for the big signal, the big shove but no such luck.

Just dark as sin now under the stars and plenty of that afoot but nothing to do with me. So I gave it the gas and raised some dust, made the on ramp in a flash and joined the highway one more time. And never looked back.

CROOK'S REMORSE

I lay chest high on the bed and it was just the dark and me, the one of us mute like in the big, heavy books and the other one stumbling, dumb, feeling for all the world as though an immense ocean rocked his insides. A tidal urge that begged to drag me out. A world unto myself, as it had always been. Always. Within that rectitude I lay waiting for the sun. Sunrise would make it 6:45 where Marie was. I would call her sometime after that. Which left a couple hours of dead peace, the mind on loan. That I would take, no matter the terms.

Out of somewhere though this sucking sound like foam and bathwater make on their way down the drain, circling their way to hell. The sucking sound of my heart slogging along in time to this tune, this disastrous little melody that I took to whistling whenever the roof and walls were on fire and caving in. The Loser's Lullaby I called it at the time, before I put it to bed and locked the door one night late, killed it for good I thought in a smash-up I recall was long on whiskey and short on tears. My soul and I, thrashing it out. And though that night had lied, I was still within its thrall. But to hell with that night, I figured.

"You buried it once, Maddock. Burn it this time. Or eat it. Nothing comes back from the bung hole."

"Screw you twice, buddy," I said, and I meant it…but I was fried.

That was when the whistling began. This jaunty little tune with squeezebox accompaniment and the quicksilver clatter of spoons. Clackity clackity clack went the spoons, a soft and soothing jingle like the Sandman makes. The melody starting me to drift so that I shut my eyes and settled deep. From whence began a weary sort of remembering…

It was from a time when all was green, even the black shadows were green. The sky was freedom and it was home over your right shoulder. The earth and even the faithless wind smelled of home. Someday. Surely.

And icy avenues, you remember the kind, the trees bare and the streets empty and muffled from the cold. Remembering the sound of your shoes on gray pavement…cold and empty windows glaring street ward through dark and leafless trees, the dark black ice on ice-covered tines and the sound your shoes made echoing from porches and walls and garage doors open to the world. You remember, don't you?

'Maybe, maybe not,' I said. I shook my head, tired of fighting.

"No lies tonight. Just peace," I bargained.

Remembering when you knew where it lay, the line, and never strayed much over. The line was fairly clear to everyone, but some went over. But not Maddock. Not the Ace. Too clever. Too sharp. But no line now, no more.

"No more lies, no more divide," I echoed, drenched as I was in an infinite sea. Such teeming life in a drop of water, the universe a solitary ocean. All one again, alone.

"Find your place in line, Maddock," came the words, at long last the words and with the words I slept. Slept the fine peaceful sleep of one who has stopped listening, stopped believing, no such thing as hope. A man-child swathed in the antipathy of cold, bitter truth. A free man, but for the chains. Forged and hammered by a duplicitous mind, corrupted and made fast by one's own hands.

I slept hard and deep, a gamble now as the eyes so gently closed. Rather like the lion or the lamb. Warily. Seeing unclearly through to a bad ending, one of death and blood, as through a fog, as though a life, long past. Seeing none too clearly yet hearing absolutely the bottom of the well. About the size of a thumbnail at arm's length - about the size of my chances.

But sleep. You're gonna need it where you're going. A short crisp burst through the light. Your thirty seconds in the spot. Till they give you the hook, buddy…and buddy, you're gonna take it.

You'll be alone again, as if anything could ever change. As if alone were a condition rather than a fait accompli. Ah yes! To write the rules and hold them to it. Now there's a dream worth dreaming…like water in the cistern: cool, blue and clear. Like the bud of a rose, begging you turn away. Or the laughter of wind in your face, the wind free while you stand rooted, an empty barn abandoned. As though opposed…

"I'll take my chances," came the words and with the words I rolled quickly from the bed. Wandering as in a fog, I stretched slowly to buy more time, tousled my hair with both hands, waking. Ah, morning's light. Such patience while the world has slumbered.

"Welcome home Kid, we missed you," I said to no one in particular. Just tossing a line and watching it coil. A bit like the giddy banker locked in the vault. All those nickels and dimes taking his air.

"How the hell are you?" someone said for laughs, and this time I meant it. This time everyone was home. Fine, just fine came the reply, but only in my head, just barely in my head.

I grabbed a smoke from the bedside table and made it over to the vanity. I started the four-cup coffee maker, the executive model they stash in all the finer rooms, dangle in front of the salesmen. That and a t-bone will get 'em to the next town.

Coffee simmering, I lit the cigarette and puffed on it while striding to the eastern window. Brushing the curtains aside, the sky was that orange and red which promises everything before it turns gray again and the blush has left the rose. Still, a fair start to things I always figured. A couple good deeds, next thing you know its lunchtime. Not exactly Murderer's Row and a bushel of laughs along the way. Maybe even rogue's remorse or love if you were so inclined and the occasional lawn party or two if you were not. A romp in the stables with Agatha, sultry maven of the horse crowd, or bourbon on ice in the Stratolounger, flipping the dial. Whatever you want to call it. A day. A life? Somehow you got your share.

The way I got mine. Coffee and cigarette at hand, I settled for bourbon, the bonded kind, and dug out my old buddy the pint. Best friends all these years and now Marie, the woman, was muscling in.

I felt sorry for my little chum and made a toast to the good times, to the memories. To our perfect life together.

Curtains thrust balefully aside, staring into a smoldering dark, I bade my little friend farewell.

"Here's to the one that got away," I said and shuddered while it all ran down.

THE BIG PRIZE

I showered quick and made more coffee, loaded up the car. I kept the duffel with the goods on the bed, but the rest I threw into the trunk and onto the backseat. It made a fine mess – the shotgun in the trunk with the suitcase and boots and the box of booze. On the backseat was the attaché that held my personal effects along with the stolen hard drive and laptop that were smothered by a jacket and a sweatshirt I threw over them for looks. Under the driver's seat I shoved the automatic and the duffel would ride shotgun. That way I could finger the money while the cops were reloading.

I locked everything down and went back inside. I wanted a cigarette and coffee before I called Marie. But the mind wanted none of that, so I strode across the pavement to the motel office and grabbed the morning press. It was 6 a.m. according to the wall clock above the front desk of the Wagon Wheel motel, located on the highway out of town, Plainview, Texas.

I grabbed a sweet roll and banana from the little kitchen they set up to jumpstart all the travelers. Get em on the road and out. I grabbed a milk too and headed back across, the office door flung wide open and nobody minding the desk. Just a curtain of heat hanging out front like a teen delinquent. A good day to keep driving.

I pushed on over to my room and tossed the newspaper onto the bedspread where it rolled open and barked out a headline. Seemed some public servant got caught with his hand in the jar. Imagine. Further down some cluck went off the road and further down from that I couldn't read it but I could guess.

"All the rubes that fit," I chirped while taking a sip of my coffee. I flipped ahead to the weather section and the map said hot, 105 degrees and that about covered it.

I lit smoke number nine and peeled the banana and took a bite of the sweet roll. It was apricot, a wonder they still grew them. More bang for the buck with peaches was my guess, from all my years of farming. I ate on.

By the time 6:15 a.m. rolled around, I had finished the repast, but I couldn't tell you what day it was. The newspaper knew what day it was, but the newspaper was on the bed and I was in the dressing nook staring at nothing, thinking about Marie. I had a call to make and it was my call but now it was about more than me and my tangled skein. The girl was in it now too, probably, more than likely.

"Try deep, sailor. Up to her neck."

Marie was in deep, at least if they could use her to get to me. Or if she happened to be there when the train pulled out. No witness, no problem as the saying goes.

"So hide, stupid."

You could hide I guess. Nothing wrong with wanting to keep breathing. And a big wide world. Run along the coast with the lady.

Or go undercover in Germantown, can some pickles. Course if you were male, white that narrowed the search a bit. Sooner or later, blooey as Lavon put it. Or maybe not. Maybe you just died like a fig. Dried out, no juice.

Dead and gone. Nothing special about that one. Except it was your dead and gone and you figured to spend it your way. Kick it around the lot like a rusted can even. But yours in other words The big prize if you never heard. Every lifer gets one.

So don't fold your tent just yet, Maddock. You aren't drawing to an inside straight. You only gotta be smarter than the dummies with the guns. The guys with narrow eyes.

"Sounds easy. Where do I sign?" I said and buckled Wilbur, the little .32, onto my ankle and slipped into a pair of moccasins brought along for driving. Rising to my feet before the mirrored vanity, trusted pint in tow, I tossed the reflection a withering glance.

"What a piece of work is man," I warbled and chased the thought with a belt. Wondering if the punishment ever really fit the crime. Just not certain I cared to know.

THE BIG MOVIE

It's what you do after you've learned that all is dross...that could be the log line to the movie...then just fade to black. The big movie, the big life, the big lie. Popcorn and peanuts ground to dust by the citizens tramping home to the wall-to-wall, the Kelvinator, the stainless-steel sink. Nobody waits around anymore for the credits, the lilting, dying refrain of the theme song. Gotta get them fish sticks in the oven.

Or maybe you got it wrong all these years. Dancing in the dark while upstairs the real party whirls along. Just when did you become the world's all-time biggest downer, eh Maddock? The once and former hero. Was it after Charlie bought it or before, one thousand years before?

"It all went south with the old guy's brains," I mumbled. A .22 caliber Pollack, fit to be framed. Right behind the left ear, thinking 'Watch it, don't splash the eyeball'. That would make a mess of things all right, rolling away beneath the couch.

A killer, yes, but oh so gentle, a gentle killer.

'A light touch, he had such a light touch, officer.'

'I can see that ma'am, a real gentleman, ma'am.'

Or maybe it was Evans and the Loverboy. The two-for-one special. Maybe that was what started your slide. Evans out of fear and the Loverboy for money. That's the one they'll write you up on. The two birds with one stone. You shot em, right?

"Yeah. And who says I'm sliding, anyway? It wasn't about the money. The bastard had it coming. I just pulled the plug, maybe. So arrest me."

Tell yourself. Cozy up to the fire and tell yourself anybody would a done it. Don't matter it waddles and quacks, it's still murder. And before that, the old man in Chicago, sweet revenge. No points for that in the Good Book, either.

"So I live with it and someday I die with it. That make you happy?"

And Marie, what about Marie? Think these guys care she steps in the way? So what about the girl? And what about Ev?

What about them? Surely they're off the main line by now. Evelyn anyway. But Marie draws interest. She's the coming attraction. You'll need to call Marie...

I babysat the clock on smokes and coffee until almost eight o'clock her time and then I went for the phone. I grabbed it the way you grab a slice of eternity, from the outside in and mindful of the horns. I grabbed the phone and dialed the girl. But it never rang through and after a while I cut the connection. Like cutting a vein and watching it flow. All these strange notions starting to swirl. And Marie with them, starting to fade.

I swung the duffel off the bed and walked with it over to the blinds, pulled them aside an inch and peeked out. Not a soul. I grabbed the doorknob and started to twist, halfway round when the hand went soft. It let go and fluttered away and this time I wasn't there to catch it. I felt it stroke my chin as the other hand went weak and the duffel dropped to the floor. Nothing else moved, just the hand on the chin.

Somewhere in all of that I must have been thinking. How else recall her answering machine and the greeting of only a day or so before: 'You have reached M & H Investigations,' Marie's announcement had said… 'Please leave a message for M & H…'

Just like an answering machine. Never there when you need them. Or they been turned off or unplugged or ripped from the wall.

Maybe I'll ask Marie. She ought to know. But Marie's not there either. She would have picked up the phone. Or maybe she's there but company dropped in. Mort and Chester from St. Louie, asking a few hard questions. Big friendly guys, a little touchy maybe…

STEVE MCQUEEN

First thing I did, I jacked out of there. I walked with the duffel to my car, the bag slightly unzipped, the ankle gun sliding around on top of the cash. The little .32 mostly a charm now. Like a rabbit's foot. The feeling beginning to build that you never have big enough balls or powder beneath them.

I backed around slow but left the lot in a hurry, taking the frontage road at fifty and skipped onto a county road the first chance I got. It was a wide-open farm road heading south. I punched it to seventy and let her pick up speed. I eased my grip on the steering wheel and began to breathe again, one more time at last. Along with the rush had come this need to focus and I ran the glass down and listened to the bugs in the fields and felt the first humid wave of morning wash over. Trees, brush, green everywhere. Ground fog crawling into gullies. Small birds flying low and liking it. Everything waking beneath a golden promise.

"And why not? You might make another day yourself," I said.

Driving fast on a county road heading south, out of sight but parallel to the Interstate. The scenery flowing by at speed, reminding me of all the fun I missed since Charlie stepped off. The drives in the country to remember. The drives to nowhere, letting the mind flow where it will, rolling down a ribbon of stone. Just remembering like it was only the other day that Charlie called to say hello. My one good buddy. And Ev, my other pal and life was good and we had all arrived and parked on High Street in the sun.

Only now it was someone else's spot at the curb and the street was no longer High Street – more like Die Street and you never saw it coming.

"I saw it. So here we are."

So here we are, a fistful of nothing for cards. Take a peek, Lucky. You always did like games of chance. See what the wind blew your way.

"Uh-uh. I ain't gonna play that game right now."

Instead, I drove on and fast but all the while I was formulating. If the game runs linear there is *a priori* a next move. Don't matter its knight or pawn, just move the piece and make it lethal. I guess what it was…I'd got over dodging around with these guys. What I wanted now was to act.

I pulled off the road at the first gas stop I found, a junction store that backed onto a field of alfalfa. A crossroads in farm America. Gas pumps rising from an ocean of gravel and a solitary cane-backed chair leaning empty, inviting, lolling on its hind legs against the pop machine they plugged in out front to bait the loungers. Keep 'em from hanging around inside, messing with the trade.

Where the front door yawned open a golden-haired dog lay half in, half out of the entry. Asleep but for a single eyebrow arched in a kind of watch dog acknowledgment. A warm sun was edging closer, taking its time, fixing to climb the golden dog's belly.

Toward the fence line hoppers were clicking and flitting about, jazzed up with a heat that was rising fast now with the hour. On the near side a pair of cottonwoods were locked in a palsied trembling, while beneath them a pay phone loitered, cool within the languorous shade they cast. The pay phone's door hung open, the receiver dangling on a silver thread, pushed round its circle by a breeze. While all around there came this frenzy of bugs flying everywhere in haste through the heat. And a buzzing, buzzing, buzzing sound.

I parked at the pumps and made my way to the pay phone. For some odd reason I tucked the 9mm into the waistband of my jeans, with the polo shirt pulled out for cover. Joe College with a real hard one. And I was wearing shades, too, the Hollywood kind. I looked like Steve McQueen but was feeling more sort of pissy, like Genghis Khan. What it was, I was sick and tired of running from these guys.

I needed to make a call and dug for coin and put one into the slot and listened as it trickled down, reminding me of an hourglass with the sand whirring through and the course of our lives. Like golden thread wove into time, all of it vanishing into the fabric.

Just standing at a crossroads the whole gone world spread away and no end to that and never would be and it gave me a kind of flinch. A shiver of remorse for all the endings that never would, the beginnings that never had. So that I told myself there could be no better time. And with that notion there came an almost dizzy feeling, but I went ahead and dialed anyway, and that saved me I guess…if anything ever does.

SEMPER FI

First thing I phoned Ev's number...Dolly's that is, but the girls weren't home and I was running out of places to call. Lavon and the gang were back in Oklahoma, he and Dolores, that match made in heaven. And Sara and Bear back with family and I had no clue how to reach them. Directory assistance?

'Yeah, can you give me the White Crow's, please?'

Part of the big plan I maybe neglected, what with all the excitement. For beat-up, hard drinkin' and forgettin' there's no place like Amarillo.

Which left the Prairie View motel and a call to the deskman who didn't much care and why not? We were almost friends going on twelve hours now and I felt like talking. To whom didn't matter. Nor did it matter particularly when Trey answered on the third ring, way above his station in life.

"Good morning, the fabulous Prairie View," he said. "This is Trey speaking."

"You been kicked upstairs, Trey?" I asked.

"A slot opened up when Willoughby got his ass handed to him. You should have stuck around, Mr. Maddock. It got wilder than a tornado."

"Willoughby make out?"

"He's going to be alright. He'll be dining in the hospital this evening if you'd like to drop by."

"I'm afraid to ask…"

"The short version - some guys wanted to find you and Mr. Willoughby refused their very generous offer on account of hotel privacy rules. They worked him over fast and printed out all the phone and registration records and receipts. They were gone inside of 5 minutes. They're like bloodhounds Mr. Maddock and they got your sock."

"What do you make of it, Trey?"

"Damnedest thing I ever seen. You show up and the Panhandle goes Red Alert."

"Tell you what, Trey. I'm putting you down for a hundred. You're worth more and you'll get it later on, but right now I need some phone numbers and I need someone to watch my back."

"You're the boss," he said.

So I gave him the number for the Dolly Lama and also some idea about Bear and Sara and Lavon and Dolores. I needed to stay in touch with them as well. I filled him in a little. But only what he needed to know. It was pretty simple really.

"We're the good guys, Trey. Don't get me wrong, cops are good guys too. For the most part. Only we want to keep them out of this affair."

"The way you say it makes sense," Trey said.

"And the hundred don't hurt either."

"If there was ever any question, the hunderd sort of smoothes it over," Trey replied.

"Another thing, Trey. If you slip with these guys the fall is hard. You think you made a deal with these guys and they already started the meter. It always runs out, Trey."

"I'll be mindful of that, Mr. Maddock. As far as making deals, we already had one, you and I."

"It's a cynical world Trey, all a man's got is his word."

"*Semper Fi* as Lavon puts it. What does that mean, anyway?"

"It's from the Marines. It means 'Always Faithful'. Least it did this morning at dawn."

"Maybe go ahead and wire me that money, Mr. Maddock. I think I might be buying a gun."

"Just Maddock, Trey. You still got my credit slips, take the number and draw a couple hundred to the motel. Get a pocketsize .380 and fill it with hollow points. Just try and never pull it."

"You got my word on that. And what about you?" he asked.

"I'm gonna make like the wind, Trey," I said.

And I did. I hung the phone on the hook and took my own sweet time strolling back - kicking the dirt, listening to the quiet the birds filled with their twittering. Birds everywhere above in the cottonwood trees, a whole village peering down, watching the poor dope shuffle to his car. Maybe they counted me out. I hoped so. I hoped they all counted me out.

"Let 'em all dream," I growled. "They'll find out soon enough what just got started."

PLAN NUMBER THREE

Floydada was the next town south, though not exactly south but south enough. When I jumped off the frontage road, I thought I was running parallel to the Interstate, but I'd caught the road to Floydada instead. It was a lucky break and it made my day. Floydada was this one-horse town and all the horses but mine were parked at the diner. I looked at my watch and it said 8 a.m.

I rolled slow into the outskirts and took a couple right turns off the main drag and circled back and checked it out. Just another Panhandle town of pale, polished grass, not green but thread-bare lawns behind chain-link fences and tricycles dangling off the porches. Mom and Dad's America. Exiting town on the other side was a small gas station with two bays and a couple heaps parked in the gravel alongside and one jutting out in back of the joint. The one out back was finished in primer and the others were in various stages of undress. Someone's hobby had turned into a chore.

I got gas again although I didn't need it and pulled a pop from the ice box they made of a wash tub and took my loot to the counter.

All the bottles were capped and the church key with the bottle opener was tied to the counter with string and snugged up against the cash register. They'd took sugar off the honor system.

"How much it cost to pop this," I said to the fellow reading the magazine on a stool behind the counter. He looked to be in charge.

"Seventy-five cents everyday but Sunday," he says.

"How much they on Sunday," I said.

"We're closed Sunday, Praise the Lord," he said and smiled.

"You all do paint and body work around here?" I asked. I was beginning to drawl, drenched as I was in friendliness.

"Not usually in that order," he said. He didn't laugh outright, just quietly snickered.

"What would you say I leave this one in your bay for a day or two while I shop a car in Lubbock. Maybe give me an estimate on painting it imperial green for my boy. It's his favorite color and he graduates this summer."

"We might need that bay."

"You need it three hunnert dollars worth?" I asked. He grinned and his teeth shined like a brand new day. He shook his head side to side. I put three bills on the counter and he still hadn't got up to pop my soda.

"Hook is, I need a ride to Lubbock an' I want the pop free."

"You drive a hard bargain," he said. "Mister...?"

"Mr. Smith," I said and watched him lift the three big ones off the counter.

"I'll just be a minute, Mr. Smith" he said and flipped the open /closed sign and locked the register. He popped my soda then and followed me out and shut the door tight. He shooed his dog inside.

"We'll be back in a flash, Herbert," he said but the dog was down already in the dust of the wood floor, eyelids clammed shut.

"That's a fine dog," I said.

"You just keep amazing me, mister. You wanna jump in that truck?"

"From here?" I asked. We was ten yards away. I looked at him and grinned. He spit tobacco and held out his hand.

"The names Winston but you can call me 'Stupid'. Everbody else does." I watched him grin again and load a toothpick and we shook hands and climbed on board the pickup.

"It's a pleasure to meet you, Winston," I told him as he turned it over and revved it once and it hummed like a watch.

"She's like my old lady. Don't look like much but man does she run."

I nodded then and off we took. One or two words and fifty miles later we pulled into Lubbock. I had him set me down in old town and told him I'd see him in a day or so. He said 'Okay' and made the next right out the way we'd come. I watched him go. Then I took off myself in a northerly direction, sun burning the shoulder and on down my back, sort of sleepwalking the dusty avenue. But the mind was working, working. I was somewhere in the middle of Plan Number Three. The one where you leave the shack a free man, laying down a cold trail. Where you buy yourself a future and bury the past.

That often hatched but rarely fledged plan for all the marbles…

MADDOCK

I walked into the Rexall and found an empty booth and ordered the cheese sandwich with chips and pickle and a soft drink they made from syrup at the soda fountain. I had a banana crème pie alongside that was so good it made me wonder why I never went straight.

While I ate, I studied the roadmap and tried to estimate how far Mutt and Jeff had got or whether they had even cleared Plainview yet with all the backtracking and checking they had to do to follow me. They sure ate a lot of ground up fast getting to Amarillo and tracing me there. Course it was pretty much a straight line and me lighting the way with a flare in my ass. Trey was right though; they were like bloodhounds.

After the sandwich I walked the block and a half of Main Street, looking in the shops, just stretching, enjoying the air. Studying the roadmap had given me the idea I might have a chance all right. A slim one maybe, but a chance and that was plenty enough to carry me.

I skipped over to the opposite side of Main and walked west to the dealership and asked the salesman how the paperwork was coming. The paperwork was coming along fine and the shag boys were finishing the clean job and everybody standing around, trying to catch a glimpse of the dope that paid cash for a two-year old sedan, sight unseen, with seventy-five thousand on it, good rubber, the paint a deep navy. Some beater from the government fleet or the county or from some insomniac chasing some circus from hell. But the deep blue pool of the navy, you could lose yourself and I aimed to give it a really good try.

Orville came out carrying the title and the keys and with a big wide grin like he just won the lotto. Swimming in the glass behind him was everybody in the showroom. I was the two-headed boy. The glue sniffin' city man. Catching the keys in my left hand they made that sort of chink chink sound of spurs. I grabbed Orville's mitt with my right.

"Go have a helluva night, Orville," I said. "You earned it." I shook his hand and let it go.

"You made my month Mr. Smith and it was all so painless. A cash deal, too."

"Easy come, easy go," I said while Orville stood there grinning, clasping his hands. He didn't look like he would ever sleep again.

"You got a sister?" I asked and climbed into the car.

"Not so you'd know it," he said. "She ain't even got her horns yet."

"Maybe next time," I said and laid a patch in the lot and swung out onto Central Ave. I was feeling my oats.

An orange sun burned low in a sky flaring quickly to yellow. Tar reared from the pavement, darting about, black like obsidian, veining the cement roadway. A couple crows startled up, gliding, cawing, rising with the heat. The boss bird glanced my way and gave me the eye.

Another hot one settling in as I ran up the glass and switched on the air and looked for a liquors. This day was shot all to hell and one way only to stop the bleeding. Not that dying wasn't an option.

I pulled over at the A-1 package store and parked along the curb and went inside and grabbed a couple pints. One for sippin' and one for mixing. The sipper was 100 proof.

"Can I make it back to Floydada before sundown?" I asked the old guy at the register.

"Depends which one you be drinkin," he smiled. He was a handsome black man with sorrowful eyes. He ran a tidy little shop.

"I think I'll be sippin' the hundred," I said.

"You halfway home already, brotha," he said and let go with the smile. He dropped the pints into a paper sack and handed them over.

"Johnny Law's all over that road."

"I'm wise to him now," I said and left him a 'much obliged' and turned from the counter. He went back to sorting change in the cash drawer. He didn't give it a whole lotta extra thought. Just the chik chik of coins as I pulled the front door shut.

I climbed back on board and headed out for Floydada, feeling like I owned the world. Enough to shoot the moon anyway, but it wasn't moons I was fixing to shoot and that was a black hole I wasn't real anxious to stick my head in.

"You poor sombitch, how'd you wind up here? Was it luck or were you just born stupid."

'I guess I was just born, Stupid.'

I flicked on the radio and the shag boys had left it set to the local country western station and the volume was up. Steel guitars and a rocking chair beat. They was playing "My Bucket's Got A Hole In It" until the station went to commercial and the disc jockey began to sell farm stuff and foot softeners. He had this real sincere voice:

"You dogs keeping you from getting your share? What you needs is Blue Moon crème. Take it from me, folks. Blue Moon. It works."

I pulled the sippin' stuff from the sack and took a sip. Then I took another and it was oh so easy.

"No more drinks 'til you got a plan," I ordered. Like I didn't have a plan. I had a plan. I was gonna blow 'em away two at a time.

"Just keep sending 'em," I said and took a long, wet swig at the fences.

Truth was, ever since Amarillo I knew I'd been kidding myself. A mob like this bunch, powerful as they were, well you either play ball or you're out. Me, I grabbed the first base bag and ran with it. Naturally they followed. And this wasn't shoplifting the corner drug either. Like I told Trey, with these guys the fall is hard.

"And your point? Get to the point, Maddock."

Point is. Point is I never liked the killing part. I thought I left that over there and so did Charlie and that was the point. That was the promise. That we would leave it lay. You remember, don't 'ya? Tell me you remember.

"Sure, I remember."

Like yesterday. Stepping off the charter, disembarking San Francisco and the tarmac hotter than jungle ever thought of being. The heat all jangly like cheap guitars and Charlie turns to me, shades, short sleeve madras shirt from some flop in Thailand. Second and last tour and smiling as always, thinking about what he wanted to say. No drum roll, no big message either. Just free as the wind behind his smile when he says to me, "Now all we gotta do is breathe." Shaking our heads with the wonder of it.

And I remember smiling to myself, thinking, 'Amen, brother', and how lucky to be young and everything sounding so easy and maybe it was, yet now somehow it had all got harder.

So I dug for the field manual but maybe I tossed it along the way - or maybe I just skipped that chapter. No matter. You knew the Corps had an answer for that one too. You could read it through the blindfold. Lock and load was what it said.

TIME WILL TELL

The next stop back was Floydada, at Ace's Place, the name of the gas station Winston inherited from his old man, Ace.

"What happened to old Ace?" I inquired.

"No one knows, they never found the body. Everybody just figures he's dead. But not enough to throw a party," he said.

"He must have been well loved."

"I never knew the man. Named me after a cigarette," he spat, and I let that one wander.

"Can you open the bay?" I asked him. "I got some stuff in the trunk I'd like to get out." We walked together to the outer bay door and he raised it up.

"Just pull it down when you're through," he said and headed for his truck. "I'm late for supper."

"Save me some gravy," I hollered as the door went thunk and he was quickly long gone, making the corner. I had the place to myself.

I popped the trunk and uncovered the shotgun and the sack with all the money and the two boxes of loose booze bottles and the suitcase with all the disguises. I moved the shotgun and a box of shells to my other car and two bottles of the hard stuff. Then I grabbed another bottle and a bundle of the cash, ten thousand tricks nestling softly within the band. The cash like a doorstop - you didn't give it much thought, but handy to have around. I grabbed a carton of smokes too, and that just about sealed it. I closed the trunk and pulled the bay door down.

Then I sat in the car and wondered what the future had in store. I drank and I smoked, no hurry at all. Like a gentleman.

I ran the seat back and put my head on the headrest and listened to the country western tunes that flowed from the mouth of the radio. I watched the birds and listened to the leaves lift in the breeze and I wondered about that too. I wondered if I was already dead or just barely alive or whether any of it mattered. While I was wondering, I pulled the 9mm from under the seat and jerked around with it. Out popped the clip, back and forward went the slide, back in went the clip, lower the hammer, flick the safety. Like a joker cracking knuckles and just as irritating. Over and over, a bad guy's worry beads. And that made me wonder some more.

"Man, how did all this come down? And does it really matter?"

It matters or you wouldn't be stuck on it. And 'no way to end' was the tripping point. Like there was 'a way to end' and I was gonna deliver it to the masses. After I did 20 to life, of course, with no chance of parole. Or just did dead and saved everybody the heartache.

"You gonna sit here countin' your eggs or you gonna crack some?" I piped. Like I could count. Like I had a choice…

You always got a choice, boy. It's called the back door. Leave it all where it lay, every snake for hisself. You could play that card.

"Not going to happen, Maddock. Not this evening. This shuffle we're gonna deal from the top. It's the big closing scene. A juicy part you been rehearsing since daddy gave you the door."

A brief little soliloquy that left me quite dry. So I took a pull on Betty the Bottle and that changed the subject, sending my mind back to where I skidded off the road. No hairpin turn, either. Straight and flat as the eye could see…and I walked to the edge and peered over and there was the plunge. The big dive into the now and everlasting evermore. And it didn't seem like you'd ever come down. But they were wrong, all of them, shortsighted, though the bottom was deep.

"So, you got it figured out, eh big boy?"

A day or so ago it was all about the little dancer Leah and her tough luck story and the legend of Maddock, the itinerant hero. But now all the bugs were loose and everybody with galoshes is front and center, slipping and sliding on the linoleum.

"Didn't Momma tell you it could turn out like this?"

Yeah, she did, probably, but I was never much for listening. Except that little voice in my head. Ding-a-ling-ling it says, you ready to cowboy up? Like I gotta be asked.

"I'm ready." Just don't know what to expect. Fire or flood or brimstone. And brimstone, I got no recollection of that one, but I can smell it from here. Sweet sulfur spells trouble anyway you carve it.

Well, the door is over there and everyone steps through - single file or arm in arm. Always wondered what was on the other side though. You can't help but wonder. Course you ask the smart guys, they all chirp the same song.

Time will tell, the graybeards croak. Time will tell.

MELVIN AND THE HAYSTACK
(BAD BID'NESS)

I beat it back to Plainview in a hurry and picked up my tail at a balmy motel on the western outskirts, the ragged edge of cotton country. They looked pretty much the way you would expect. A big bulky guy in a blue suit, similar to a meat locker or a billboard in size. He rode shotgun with his arm outside the car window. The little guy was all wire, fidgety, as if he had a permanent itch, a skin condition. His was the head of a ferret, but the big guy was more that of a gallon milk jug. All things being equal, I would have to shoot the big one first. The little thin guy, you'd probably miss him with a scattergun, you'd have to gig him like a frog and stake him where he lay. Oh yes, it was going to be some kind of party.

I picked them up at a cheap motel on the western side of old town, the easiest side to start if you weren't big on work and only got into the killing jag on account it didn't require much more than a healthy disregard for the Sixth Commandment.

They were pulling out in a gray sedan, on their way to the next likely place I might have stopped. That or they were gonna book it and eat a late lunch at a lounge and pick up the available talent and do whatever they did to the ladies and called it love. A pair of real lookers. Course, if you were that kind of meal you'd be hard pressed to choose a favorite. Unless you were the sort of bony type, and that x'ed out the big guy, the bruiser. The big guy, in my mind, I was already calling him Haystack. I was looking forward to blowing his brains out.

The little guy, I didn't care for him much either. I could see a 9mm spinning him like a card. When I thought about it my mouth arched in a weird sort of smile, all on its own. Like the mind was away, skipping rope. I shook my head. I'd have to put another two in him for good measure. One of those guys you gotta burn to make sure. Man, I was getting cold.

The way I framed it, these guys were done already…it was them or me and I got the first jump. The more mess I made of them the better was the way I looked at it. Nothing personal, but you couldn't miss your one shot and just drift with the tide and that got me to thinking. Maybe there was a different way to pull this off. A better way. And that struck me as funny, how quick you can shuffle when everybody's got a knife.

I followed them for another few blocks and watched them pull into a motor court you couldn't pay me to stay in. Two minutes and the big guy wedged back into the car and they dropped back onto the avenue. Then they did it again. And again. They stopped at a drive-in and got a couple floats and drove out. Over and over, like a leaky faucet. Like a two-man locust plague. And they just kept on moving, eating up ground. It was something to see, the professionalism of a couple of low-watt hoodlum killers. Fascinating, like watching a snake swallow an egg, and I was gonna bring the shovel down. Smash it flat or slice it wide. Made no matter now, this death business.

They pulled in for dinner at seven on the south end of town. They had covered it all, every rat-hole and shithouse. It was something to see. And Haystack did all the footwork. Melvin, the little rat guy, was the brains, I guess. Their next stop would be Lubbock, but first it was tits and grits at the gentleman steakhouse they saw advertised on a billboard off the southern exit. Or maybe they inquired along the way, the Haystack always dreaming about food, licking his lips and asking: 'Hey, where's a good place to eat? I like a big hearty meal before I choke somebody's guts out and leave him in a ditch.'

A pair of ice-cold killers wandering through Texas, foraging for food and these two settled on The Roper, a dance club, and rolled in and parked beneath a sign that featured a cowgirl wearing not too much in the way of clothes. She was about twelve feet tall. She was inviting the cowboys to 'Come on In and Get Some'. The boys didn't need much coaxing. Steak and tail. Haystack and Melvin piled out and stretched.

I drove past and did a U-turn and parked at a laundromat on the eastern side and next door was a Chinese food joint and I went in and caught a window seat. It was cool inside and dark with the Chinese lanterns and the red everywhere. I had them bring me the combo plate with iced tea and paid up right away. Then I just waited and watched while I waited and watched. Like a dog and his tail or some circus boy strapped to the maypole, round and round.

After dinner I had a Mai Tai and then a Midori on ice. No smoking so I paid for the drinks and stepped outside and struck a pose along with a match. I lit up and walked to my car as the twins stepped out of The Roper. Haystack was real light on his feet, gorged and happy. Melvin had a hard stool for a master. Didn't look like he ever smiled. I studied them with field glasses so I'd know, even in my sleep. Shoulder to shoulder in the car they looked like clay pigeons. They probably thought they had the upper hand. All the while I was circling closer.

I watched them through binoculars, and it was easy to patch the whole thing together. Melvin the rat licked his lips, wanted to go back inside and do some drinking. Haystack was ready to move on, get a bed in Lubbock and watch the tube. He'd had his pleasure. They passed a bottle back and forth and squabbled. Melvin with hard, wet, metallic eyes and the Haystack all jowly and dense. Mobville's finest.

I thought about blowing them away then and there with the scattergun, leaving a smoldering pile in the lot, but that didn't really solve anything. The guy who pushed the buttons would only send two more. Or three. So it had to be an accident to buy me some time, move out of the crosshairs, maybe permanent. Or go so dark they gave it up as debt unpaid. Uncollectible.

Meantime I sat in the car and matched the Haystack shot for shot. Melvin was back inside, and I had the Haystack to myself, talking to him all the while. We were drinking buddies, getting to be real chums.

When the sun was well down, I could see him plain and gray in the lights of the parking lot, snacking and reading the newspaper beneath the dome light of the car. Poor stupid Haystack. He was dead already.

And maybe I was too and just didn't know it. Maybe all this time I was already gone, or just enough if there is such a thing, but I don't think there ever was. How else could a wisp of nothing dream up the mayhem I had my hands so deep within? Or if it was only a dream the nut that was dreaming me was gone to the nth. And that hat would never quite fit I supposed, and I guessed I would have to ask Sara White Crow about that one someday. She was the bird to ask when it came to dreams and distant drums.

And I thought about Sara then and Bear and Lavon and Dolores and Trey and Willoughby and the rest of that gang. And what a jumble I had made of things, starting with the old man in Chicago, and Evans, and the Loverboy. I thought about them all and it seemed a runaway train I'd shoved them on with no way to pull them off. All I could do was wave bye-bye as they jacked into the canyon.

And Marie and Ev popped up next and I was tired of it and had no answers for them either. Least not the ones that would have mattered.

So it was what it was and I pulled another drink and rubbed my eyes and thought about my little green bike and my little dog Snoop and all that tangled mist from yesteryear. It did me no good. My own mind had fled.

In its place was a foul taste I didn't dare swallow. Not the shipwreck a load of booze leaves in its wake either, but the moldering taste of fear. Fear from inside, never from without, and one way only on this foul little planet to be rid of it. So much I knew but not much more. Which gave me a big case of the wets.

I was up to my socks in tears when Melvin reappeared, pushing open the front door of the club and cinching his pants and rounding the fender of the car. Haystack was sound asleep, a little pink cherub blowing feathers. I had all night, I could've put the shotgun under his chin and given him a lift but I didn't. I wanted to take them out together now. Plan number four and a real doozy.

Melvin turned on the headlights and tossed out a butt and powered up the side glass window. Haystack straightened himself and hung an arm out his side and away they went. I gave them half a block to the highway and then I cranked it over and set off after them. They were out of sight by the time I turned off the headlights and entered the onramp.

Once we made the Interstate night overtook our little caravan. The lights of the city gone well to earth. No moon above. No fateful tremor in the heavens. No smattering of stars. Just a snake with glowing eyes and silent tail, slithering down a highway of stone. Dark as sin on a sleigh ride to hell.

MURDER MAN (MARKER 570)

It wasn't something you thought about and then one day there were three. Well, well. And now it was the easiest thing in the world to conceive. Except sleep. It all came flooding back when your guard was down. But I didn't like to talk about it on the waking side. I didn't like the images.

So down went the shotgun barrel in the passenger foot well and I put the 9mm on the seat above, started a cigarette glowing and set a cup of ice filled with the clear strong stuff into the cup holder and started the car. I was big as King Tut.

"Tut the Nut," I whispered to my gaggle of friends.

Amidst the 38 miles before you found the outskirts of Lubbock there arose some ten or so overpasses with those squat concrete pylons that collect the dead. On most occasions they merely collect the parts. Big plan number 4, the doozy, I meant to force Melvin and the Haystack smack into the center of one, head-on, and I liked my chances. Darkness, you understand, would be my friend. The guns...

the guns were there in case I had to finish it. Which was bad. The whole premise being to make it appear an accident. For the cops and everybody. Buy me enough time to floss. One way or another though they had to die and that was why the booze rode shotgun.

The highway had long gone quiet, waiting on the big show. A car or two approached from the opposite direction, passing us well across a broad, dark median. Melvin and Haystack rolling along at seventy-five and I trailing them near and just far enough. Melvin, the rat boy, had stuck their car on cruise control and was holding them sure and steady and someday I was gonna wanna thank him. Just not on this trip, buddy. Not on this go-round. But I owed him and trailed him just so, the eyes blind to a future that was closing fast. But who's future one might inquire? Theirs or mine?

Gritting my teeth at the thought of it, the mug stretched tight at the corners, I waggled my neck to stay loose and rolled my eyes. But I never glanced at the rearview, just hung on to the wheel and let everything flow straight on down the centerline. I didn't want to spook myself, flare up yellow in the night. Instead, I feathered the gas pedal, closing on them a yard or two a minute. Slowly, slowly, a leaf gone lazy on the stream of time. In the distance, one could just barely make out the rumble of the falls. Oh, brother.

I flew off the interstate first chance I got and turned on the headlights while jetting down the offramp and did a rolling stop through the stop sign and rose up the entrance ramp on the other side and onto the Interstate once again. As far as the boys were concerned, just another brush salesman, late for the buffet. I stayed back a quarter mile and timed it with the little clock in my head, just to be sure. It timed out all right. I poured myself some moon juice and fingered the auto, like a nice boy holding his crank.

Twenty-three miles out from Lubbock I started the count. I counted the one-mile signs and the reflectors, even the thumps of the expansion joints in the pavement. I was pretty keyed-up. I was at that range where one could clearly make out the Haystack - in my mind at least I could see him plain, but the mind will play tricks. Once fear has moved in. Once cold fear has bought the house next door.

And a strange thing began to happen. You know it was dark when Marie began to pry into my thoughts that way, though she didn't belong there and I refused her and would not let her in. I told her to stay out and spit her from my mind violently and with some anger and when I glimpsed the rearview this time the pieces were all there. Moving, lying, sick at heart. I tore my eyes away fast, only not fast enough. The part of you that dies took a blow right then and went down, down, but somehow you always get up. I lit another smoke and let go the handle of the gun. I needed both hands on the wheel.

So you run your eyes a last time round the circle, take in all the faces, those one million dramas in life number five. And the faces fly past, and Charlie's went by and it was always red. The rest were a sandy gray, but Charlie's was always red.

'Rhymes with dead,' I whispered, but only with my eyes.

Haystack, his name was, Haystack I had called him…no matter his name, I hadn't forgotten. Only my own it seemed. I'd neglected to remember my own…

You forgot what it was that jumped you here, didn't you fella?

"Just kill 'em."

'Yeah.'

"The mother's want your ass."

'Just kill 'em like they never were. And you better twist it in that fucking rat boy. You better gut him.'

"Just kill 'em dead."

'Right.'

Over and over, the chances thinning out, every six miles another overpass, on the section lines I suppose. And goddamn but it got dark. The only life the one or two farmhouses passing in the distance, some abandoned, the lights bobbing here and there off the bow, drifting away from the Interstate like drifting out to sea. But I couldn't look now. I was froze and drunk and I had them in my sights. There was no way to tear my eyes away now.

'It's you or them,' I heard from below, along with a hissing sound I couldn't place. It ate at me that I couldn't place it.

'Just break the ice, eh, Maddock. Remember? You were always the one

to handle it, to put out the fire.'

Remember, Maddock? Remember? Big hero?

"Screw them and screw you, you piece of shit. You do it or I'll do it now. You better do it you…"

Yella piece a shit.

"Ready? Are you ready to do it, you? It's all you gotta do is do it…"

…

It's mile marker 570 if you ever get out that way. This time or your next time around. Drive out on a dark night, no moon, stars I guess, I wouldn't know.

It's marker 570, but you'll smell it before you get there. Haystack and the Rat Boy and my bowels splashed on the concrete. Metal, stone and flesh. Burning rubber. The burning flesh and the glass everywhere.

You know the animals heard it and later, closer, they smelled it. I don't suppose any of them would hazard coming right in, grabbing the Rat Boy's arm and shaking it. But you gotta know, the animals, they're always hungry. Unlike us. We got plenty free time, enough to fly to the moon.

Mile 570 or thereabouts. Go see. See what you can do if you put the mind to it. The wonderful, crystal mind, with all its facets, its sharp edges. Only try and not look dead on. It's a cold heart reflecting back.

BIG SPRING

I made Big Spring that first night and checked into the Settlers Hotel downtown. The lobby was a little vacant, the lights dimmed and the atmosphere musty. It was something once, back in the old days, but now the clientele was threadbare and a little suspect. Me, I was just a red-blooded killer. On the rebound.

I had dropped Blue off in Floydada at Ace's, switched out my regular wheels and told Winston to paint her imperial green and patch the body. I told him I would send the boy along someday and left him $4000.00 cash. He took it all in stride and wished me luck.

"Best of luck, Smith," he said. He was rolling a toothpick round the corner pocket and peering in. A man of few words.

So I loaded up again and made Big Spring around midnight, driving past the Ranger and Cactus motels, the latter's sign dangling a green neon cactus with a serape and sombrero wearing Mexican leaning against it, chin on his chest resting. Standing upon red neon lettering that spelled 'Vacancy' in a faded smear that gave itself to the night. A wonder the sign still burned. A genuine pair of adobe and turquoise painted block motels that had seen better days; enjoying the gay squalor of retirement maybe, but that was forty years back. Nowadays they were all booked-up with ghosts.

"Some other time," I nodded. I had memories of my own to kill.

So I pulled into downtown, old town now and off of the old Main street into the lot and parked on the far side away from the front of the hotel, coming to rest in the dark. For some reason I was worried about the cops. Odd.

I checked in and then I hauled the good stuff up to my room. I figured to sleep a few hours then back on the road. I could smell that bonfire from here, with its flesh and blood and the gasoline smell before it all went off. My vote was for losing it fast.

I took a corner room on four for the view and threw everything on the day bed and pulled back the curtains and gazed due east. Daylight in three hours and that begged for a toast or something, so I brought out the twelve-year old label and swirled the red stuff round a water glass, watching the cascade of liquor trace the wall that held it. Captive. We were all bound, all. To those who made us, to those whom we had become. All bound to blank infinity.

"If you say so," I sputtered, somewhat casually. All the fight was gone from me now.

I started a smoke and ran water into the tub. I left the gun in the duffel this time; it was just me and the cops for now and I wouldn't shoot it out with the cops. I headed back to the bath and climbed in and slid beneath the waves and tried to numb my mind. It was a slow rise from deep down under and I was nowhere near the surface, so I smoked and drank in the tub and had a shave and washed and dried and lay on the bed in my towel and thought about all of it. But the mind didn't want to play that game and I lay like a cadaver, resting before the next class. The only thing that moved was my face, it couldn't get comfortable. It just mugged.

"You're a real cut-up, Maddock. When did you get so funny?"

Talking to myself now, a regular Chatty Cathy. I got up and turned on the tube, stood there gawking, the mind flickering from gray to black. There was nothing on, just dolls walking back and forth in the box…and me all dripped out.

"Lay on down, boy. Whatever you earned, you earned in spades."

I had a nice cough and headed for the wet bar to grab a big gulp of the red. And I needed the rest though I was a bit afraid of what I might find there. Like the black widow spider on his first date. So I lay myself down, the eyes wide open. Only then did I drift into dream. Only then did I drift into sleep…

It wasn't a thriller, in the dream there was no such animal as fate. No such animal as pain and anguish and the birds flew the way that birds will fly. There was ground under your feet too, but you wouldn't know it. And clouds in the sky…but it didn't register. What you realized…all was as it ever had been, ever was.

Course you could fly if you wanted to, but why? All you ever wanted, you had. All the love, all the peace, all the justice for all…

Marie was with me in the dream and I knew I would never be complete without her. It was the island dream all right, she and I in love the way it was meant, back in the garden times. Moonrise from a deep ocean world, Atlantis itself an exotic frame to our deep ocean love and it broke my heart, tossed me against the staves of emotion, untethered my lust so that life primeval lay its claim and I woke with a shudder.

'Dream gone' sighed the sailor and I slipped from the bed, pulled on jeans and poked around the suitcase for a t-shirt. Like every other insomniac, in town for the convention. Dressing up for the 4 am mixer.

I circled the room for a while and then I got the auto out of the duffel and hooked it into my jeans. Every day a new day the wise man whistled. I ran a hand across my chin and felt for the shave and splashed hot water on my face and wondered if I should open my eyes again or just end it right there. But the light was calling. That blessed light. I chucked the face towel into the sink.

"When in Rome," I yipped and Rome was Big Spring, Texas, hotter than dead armadillo pie in about 5 hours. Nothing but mesquite and goats for a hundred miles around. Oh, yeah, and oil, almost forgot. It was some place all right and I loaded a cigarette and struck the match. I had a puff and ambled over to the wet bar and then to the window with my breakfast fix. I leaned against the window frame and took it all in.

Gazing southeast were the highlands that overhang San Antonio, edging the Hill County, crowding the miles of broad coastal plain that run the table east to Louisiana, fanning out like a Spanish dancer's skirt. Beautiful country by night, rough and ill-tempered by day. A vestige of the last bit of hospitable country miraging off to the southwest now, running hell-bent for Mexico and dying there of thirst.

They'd built an Army Air Corp base out there in '42, the war just around the corner and the things had to land somewhere didn't they so why not where they couldn't hit nobody if they tried? That was where Big Daddy's boy pulled duty. And now his spunk was passing through under the cover of night. There's your gold for the mantle, boy.

"Not much company, are you," I sniffed, trying to break the spell. I was coming out of it fast now and pulled the curtains aside, regaled myself with the thin sheaf of light that lay golden on the sill. Ah, sunrise. That made it morning, 4:30 a.m., and time had got a big leap on things as usual.

Four stories down the dark of the concrete was lightening to gray. I moved across the room and started to make coffee. Going through the motions blind, mechanical, all the while staring somewhere deep within. This thing about Marie. All this mental business giving me fits. But Marie was real and the cops were real and Haystack and Melvin, the dead guys, were real. Everyone but me you might say, but why say anything at all.

"Well, well. Get a load of Kid Lucky. Maddock, the mad dog. Get a load of you, would ya."

Curtains drawn, gazing from the window of a once memorable hotel in a once memorable town. The stolid guy with the long memory. How well you remember, Kid.

"Knock it off, Maddock. You need to be straight with it now. It was fine before, the pot was small, a friendly game among friendly men. Now the game, you never win it, from life on down to this moment, and no hero either. If it's going to mean anything, you might want to be straight with it now. Marie needs you to be straight with it now."

And was I supposed to keep heading her direction then, drag everything to her door? Murder her too, in the process. Was that where this train was heading? And nobody at the stick, either.

"All these questions. Can't a guy have his coffee first?" I mocked. Comical, sure, but deadly serious, all the same.

"Or deadly dead, more like it. You can do dead, can't you, Maddock? Or is that a little personal, huh? Maybe time to rein things in?"

I got a grip and skipped to the duffel, spritzed my coffee with a gallon of regular. I knew how to get limber, make the wide turn. Too bad I was late for confession. But I hustled along to the windowsill anyway and took my seat for the grand opening.

Sunlight painting the distant tips of the treetops gold. Precious rays cutting through the dark. Ah, such a golden world, too bad I missed it, dropped off the trail and cut through the gorse. Bushwhacked my way to hell. Until, that is, I heard the robin sing, somewhere in the still gray of morning.

I had another cigarette and wondered why, while out in the nothing, a lonely dog barked. It was then I realized that the pointed question and I were old friends. And the answer, too, it turns out.

"It's to eat up time, dummy. Chew through 'til you get to the good stuff, the angel food cake and the harps."

"Let it be later," I whispered and watched as a cop car rolled into the lot below. He drove the long file of cars and looped around back and shot onto Main Street from the western side and kept on heading on. To rattle more locks, to illuminate the dark. I could just make his elbow hanging from the cruiser window, shoulder patch twinkling, and it turned me to gravy, gave me the shakes.

I stubbed my smoke and knocked down what was left of the juice, shoveled my kit back together and loaded more coffee. All of a sudden, I was in a big hurry. Except my hair, it was in no hurry at all. It was standing straight up, pointing at the Big Dipper. Funny what cops will do to you.

I made a scouting trip down to the car and then I climbed back upstairs to gather most of what comprised my kit and slipped quietly into the hall again. It was far to ground, but I took the stairwell just the same. All my life I took the stairwell just the same.

"Calm down, dummy," my little voice whispered, and I heeded it. At 4 a.m. and packing a gun, you listen to the boss.

Where it had appeared dark from the window of the hotel, at street level everything had gone a grey monotone that pooled all around. A dark grey smudge on dark gray slacks and I liked it that way. I stood outside the stairwell door and swept the parking lot with searching eyes that drew a blank.

No sound, too early, or else it might have been Sunday, but I couldn't remember. At least it was cool and quiet. The moon, that bitch, was full of herself, rising high and bright and cheery now, a bauble on a diamond chain of stars far above the dark side of the building. I wanted to knock her flat.

"Cut it, Maddock. Quit picking on the moon. You haven't a friend as it is."

I made a last haul of what was left to the car and popped the trunk. No dead bodies but plenty of cash. I threw the duffel inside and squashed the lid and made it snappy to the driver's side door. I got in fast.

"Now then, *senor*, I take?" the little voice said, and I tried to figure where, when, whispered 'hell yeah', turned the key and that was that. Sometimes, it's just that easy.

The car went vroom as I shoved it into reverse and wheeled her out and around. I stuck it into drive and wasted no time beating it back to the Interstate.

Like a rat with cheese and a big yellow grin, I was happy now, my tail wriggling gaily as I scurried up the onramp. But in the rear-view mirror, there was nary a whisker, there was nary a smile.

Eyes was all. Haggard eyes. Lost and found eyes, bearing a twinkle from a gallery of stars.

SOUTH

The memories, the warm ones, petered out about 50 miles on, leaving the dregs, what was left of them anyway, and not exactly breast milk…still, I wasn't planning on melting any hearts.

What I figured, the only thing I figured, was the road south, all the way to the Gulf and the Autumn Dove and her problem. If I could fix her mess, as advertised, I was free to head east along the ocean's edge, free to start fresh with Marie and all which that entailed. Or just pull off in San Antone now, set my course due east to Houston, New Orleans, the Florida Panhandle and thence to my Marie. Let the little Leah make a life of it, dancing for the boys from south of the border. It was her dime.

Yet still one call to Marie was required, I was certain, and soon, to drop out of sight, shut down the search for an office for M & H, until we knew who was gunning for me, that was all.

Free, for however long.

And a stop at the homeplace, always a part of the plan, where often I went to empty the mind, rewind the clock, begin at the beginning, sweep away the fog.

But, along with Marie and I, there was the Autumn Dove question still, which I would handle, must handle, featuring a hard-ass, bad-ass crew and their clear, simple motives – money, power, women and wine. It was what I reckoned with all these years. Easy as carving a melon and I had the knife, well stropped and silver in the moonlight. It was what I did.

And yet this other problem had crowded my mind, and it was fundamental. The question being, how was it I had come unstuck, the heart tearing away, rising higher, higher, deep red until pink almost, almost white as it sailed higher, expanding, until poof! Bang! Higher than the sun even? And back to earth.

By which I meant, 'What happened to my center?' and 'where had I lost it?' Why this blind stumble into trouble I could easily have avoided. This dance with terminal mayhem I had always side-stepped…proud of the cape work, no *Tercio de Muerte*…everything clean until now. Only now, everything a fog.

It all started with Charlie one might suppose, ran through the old man in Chicago, dead, Evans, the Lover Boy, dead I supposed, Melvin and The Haystack, dead. The whole mess of them weighing on me, so that I felt the soul-cleansing sweat lodge of the homeplace was in order. It was obvious to me, and Sara sent me there, *Hashtahli* ordered it, my walk with the People ordained it.

Due south, therefore, and solid, with a plan. South to the homeplace, where it all began.

HOMEPLACE

They came in the 1840's thereabouts, the Germans, Bohemians, Poles and Czechs, some Irish, others, whatever breed could scrape together transport, courage. Europeans fleeing the wars which never seemed to end, the famines which came regularly, the persecution and lack of opportunity of second sons and all daughters.

They landed weak, ill-spent more often than not, on the stretch of coast known as Indian Point, later Indianola, to huddle inland, to the promised land grants that often did not materialize, to the new homes of tents and lean-tos the mind's eye had embellished on the long days at sea.

Farmers mostly, and wheel rights, saloon keepers and mule skinners to haul the old country keepsakes; and men with strong backs, women the same, the young boys that walked to the harbors of the old country, no tears from the ships as their vision turned west, farmed out or heading to cousins and uncles and aunts, indentured by parents with no place for them at home.

Grampa came of age somewhat later, a boy born of this country, and married a young woman of property, rare then, and began to farm the land, to raise a crop of boys and a daughter. The way it was always done, back in the day.

In 1943, the army air cadet showed up (soon to be a 2nd Lieutenant, sharp in his uniform, silver wings), a blind date and the beautiful, leggy young girl and, as happened back then, it happened quick, the war putting urgency to the natural urgency of young love.

Soon, after the mystery of allotted time, the dates and dinners with family, the brothers and cousins and old folks had their glimpse, the walking out and hand-holding, and always the war (a check from a thankful government, if I don't make it), all the secrets that were theirs, not ours, not remembered now, and lost in the tumult of babies and duty and the new life they earned for themselves…and so they drove down the farm road together and out the gate to an awaiting world, the old folks turning away; Opa to the barn and Oma to the girl's room, now empty, to remember, a tear and heaving chest, a joy in the mystery of the old cycle of life.

… . … . .

I sat alongside the farm gate, in the borrow ditch and gazed up the hill to where the pasture flattened out, the peak of the house hidden by the grade coursing down pasture to the rear, where the best grass was, just under a mile, where it all began. The terraces crumbling now, tired of holding water, and I remembered my own tears, leaving Ma and Pop in my own way, and Mother telling me how they cried. A circle, and all things round are strong.

The old gate posts had never changed, though the gates came and went with time, the lessee's hanging their own gates now, metal, to graze the ground. And the old gate posts, green and slick while fresh and young, still solid though grey finally, dry and hard, were not going anywhere anytime soon.

Up in the field where Grampa plowed with mule, and later tractor, dropped in the small town by rail, where the main street dead ended at the cotton gin, trundled off the flatcar which stopped a short mile away, that he rode up Broadway and out to the farm, the whole community waving at the strength and prosperity they shared in common. Cotton in the early years, corn later, orchards for themselves and the gardens she tended with Mama, self-sufficient with the bartering which everyone needed to get by; some wild game but chickens and milk cows and hogs, riding the pony to the nearer settlement for flour. Taking his own sack. What a time it was.

But not her world, at least not with the war and the young women going to the cities thereabouts, joining the modern movement of the new world, no longer held by the farms and the rigid calendar of the old ways. Some stayed, but not she, not her friends, on to the city, the excitement, the men, fashions, the beating heart of the city, for love.

Some boys stayed home, some hearts left alone to farm and fret for the love lost to the times but finding truth in the work and romance again and dances, feasts where the community renewed and the old hurts were healed over, sometimes.

And I sat parked in the ditch outside the locked gate to the home place, wind making its noise in the heat, then dying, buzzards circling and the cattle bunched under trees, swatting the flies with expert tails and chewing slowly, staring out at their moment in time; dry the pasture's grass, waving at nothing, content, barbed wire at the ready, and all manner of bugs whistling and clicking.

Where it began. And I remembered the walk to the gate, past the tall canes that grew in the damp of the culvert, where the dogs sometimes got bit, and across the gravel road to the mailbox with its mystery red flag indicating outbound mail left, mail delivered. The solitary half mile back to the farmhouse, two-wheel rutted dirt road, snakes and rabbits and red ants, roadrunners, and coyotes, fearful for a boy of 10, not so much a man of 20, but wary. Chicken hawks and Mexican eagles, riding the heat. Then as now, it felt good, no other place better and true.

I swigged some water, a smile building at the warm thoughts, and grabbed the paper from Denver off the seat, the paper I picked up in San Antone, when I gassed up one more time for the run to the coast, the 80 miles due south, terminus of this phase. Some trepidation, wondering if the story was printed yet and how the story would shake out, not figuring for a proper bow on this package, but hopeful anyway. Until I reached page three.

Well, then. It seemed a certain Detective Evans (a vice dick, clean and upstanding) had taken down the animal killer of a young socialite, daughter of prominent philanthropist Dodson, the builder. Got the drop on him, and in a hail of bullets managed to plug him 5 or 6 times, close range. His antagonist had fired as well and missed… boom! boom! Guns everywhere. It wasn't yet clear how it all came together, but everyone was certain Evans did the world a favor. The DNA was a match, the story not so far-fetched given the outcome, everyone breathing a sigh of relief. Lover Boy, the dead man, was barely a footnote. I skipped quickly over his name, didn't want to even read it. Still, I felt rather sick, my hands all over this one. Again. And there didn't seem to be an end to any of it, and I sat square in the middle. Again.

Who were the two shadows at Lover Boy's apartment, one might ask? The one I shot down, the one that crawled away? I figured in a vague, denial sort of way it had been Evans and Lover Boy. I left town thinking it was so. And yet it now seemed Evans had set me up, as I always supposed he would. Were the two merely a couple of friendly boys from Chicago, brought in by Evans to throw a blanket on this one, tie me in on it, throw me on top of Lover Boy and phone it in? And where did Haystack and Rat Boy come off?

Man, my daydreams had come to an abrupt, unsatisfactory halt. I shook a rattled head and took another swig of water while thinking about the bottle. I reached under the front seat and touched the 9mm, in a friendly sort of way. My best friend, my only friend now, and I gazed up pasture one more time, but truly, I didn't see it. I heard the bugs clicking too but their buzzing buzzing didn't register. I believe I may even have uttered, 'ho-ly shit', but I wouldn't bet on it. Just tossed the paper aside as I cranked the engine over, laid a patch in the dirt and continued south.

I headed south.

COTTON PATCH

I blew down the farm road to the junction, old grey boarded shacks, sharecropper shacks some were, from the 30's, 40's as the Depression hit and then the war, land and farmhands hard to come by, first sons of fathers, hard nailed daughters. It was tough all over. But a big, strong country – hard, steel-eyed, failure not much of an option back then, though many failed. But not the whole. It held.

And the stories told, the dances at Cotton Patch, just another junction in farm country, with the cement dance floor under the stars, strung with bulbs and cars thrown here and yon, folks milling about, drinking and telling their stories too, and dancing until midnight called – gotta feed the chickens one said, got a mare about to fowl said another, all the old ways to change partners and dance on.

Bob Wills played there, San Antonio Rose, and Pete Fountain danced them round to Saints Go Marching In (or was it Peanuts Hucko) under a south Texas moon, clarinet blaring while the little boys threw rocks and chased little girls with grasshoppers, mothers catching up with neighbor friends and the men serious, the crop, you know, the War, the drought, seed corn and feeder cattle, all the secret sauce of country living, if you could call it that, and some years, well, a mighty fine life. Freedom to starve some years and pay back the note some others.

And I blew past the junction where the beer and pop was iced in the Cotton Patch store with the wooden band shell and concrete dance floor out the side still, under the same stars and I remembered. It wasn't my time but still, a young boy with no hips yet could sure hold his jeans up with a tug and be the man he was growing into. That was all.

There was grass between the cracks now, all the ranch boys and farm hands were long gone (their sons and grandsons filled the rank), the beautiful young girls also and you had to wonder was it real, what purpose served by the nights, the stars, the passion that flowed. I always thought it mattered, somehow. I had faith it mattered, somehow. It would hurt too much if it didn't.

And at the junction I made the turn south, on to Yorktown for a last fill-up, for a coffee and some donuts at the Palace. And a call to Marie, a call I was avoiding, the spill the beans call. Well, well.

So I rolled into Yorktown and gassed up at the big station with the diesels grumbling softly, all the coming and going always giving me a lift, the truckers swinging up into their cabs. They say happiness is in the business of living and working, even someone else's living and working can bring it. And all that striving always worked that way for me. And so I climbed back on board and cut across the busy street to the donut place on the other side. I parked and crunched across gravel to the door and pulled myself in.

It was almost empty inside, quiet, the early birds long set off for home, riding the coffee and sugar buzz, the only racket being the drive-thru doing land office. Nothing but a dark-haired tat-tooed looking ex-con sitting by himself in a booth, staring straight through me. He was trouble for sure, just not my problem until he waved me over. He nodded at the other side of the booth to show me consideration and waited calmly while I grabbed the donuts off the counter and stirred some cream into my coffee - I didn't want to burn my lip. The Vietnamese proprietor pushed my change across, which I dropped into the tip jar and nodded. I walked over to join my new friend.

"Haven't seen you befo," he said. "I would a remembered."

"It was a long time ago. How long you been out?"

"You see? Tha's why I call you over. Nobody round here dare even look at me. But you eye me in a instant. You didn't look away quick, neither. You read me good and fast." He was 5'7" maybe, shoulders to neck piled with muscle like cumulus clouds stacked one on the other, billowing up, just waiting to break loose. His arms were inked and up through the open collar of his five and dime shirt where the ink spouted up like a fountain, up his neck and beneath his chin, there was a spider web and what looked to be a brown recluse etched in the middle, aching to bite somebody. He had a tear at each corner of his eye and above his eyebrows some other symbols and curli-cue lettering. An iron cross. All black ink. He had a silver cap on an upper tooth that he kept running his tongue over and rough hands on the tabletop, round the Styrofoam cup of his coffee. His hair was black and blue with a Moe cut across the forehead, his hair hanging straight down. Not a little bit Native one might say.

"So tell me what you know, Gringo. What makes you so smart?"

"Well, I never been in the can, for one. Where'd you do your stretch?"

"Huntsville. I lifted weights in the yard and lifted books in the library. I learned my history. I learned to stay within my clan's own boundary, stay out of the cities. You know, my Lipan side been hangin' down here a thousand years. The Spanish come, 600 hundred years back, my other side. Six Flags my ass. Where the Apache flag, the Karankawa? We owned it all. Natives, that is."

"You owned some, you took some."

"We took Victoria once, for a few days. My clan remembers that one. That was Comanche, though."

"You gotta hold it."

"You know this town, Yorktown? We killed the sombitch, they name the town after him, and we rode on. So, tell me what you know."

"Nothing but killing and dying down here for the last 600 years. Natives first, Spaniards and French, Texians, Tejanos, Texicans, mestizos, mulattos, Mexicans, Spanish creoles, white settlers, African slaves. Only ones with any sense were the French. They cashed out early."

"I read the history. Nothing pretty before the Conquistadores, either; not much peace thereafter for any of us."

"Until now. Room for everybody now."

"If you say so, Gringo. Most of us been cleared out."

"I was born outside Cuero, thirty miles from Gonzales where they fired the first shot of the Texas Revolution. 'Come And Take It' the flag said. Kicked Santa Anna's dragoons back to Bexar. The Alamo was a little later. The execution of hundreds of unarmed prisoners,

Texian soldiers, at Goliad, other places, soon to follow. The Runaway Scrape, whole settlements bugging out."

"Better a bullet than smallpox."

"All around here was home, where the settlers from the 1830's landed, fleeing… guess what? War, slavery of a kind, the enlightened kind: indentured, farmed out, debtors or just plain orphaned by the structure of things – poverty and hunger. They landed on the coast, hauled north to the free land and then it was 'root hog or die'. Seems like everybody was getting in the way of everybody else. That's about all I know. The name's Maddock."

"I'm Bravo. Means brave…or angry. I been both."

"Want a donut, Bravo? You hungry?" I ripped the bag open and there they lay; I hadn't had a bite. It's rude to eat in front of a hungry man.

"Thanks, Maddock." He grabbed one of the two glazed and had a bite.

"I tell you what I'm hungry for. I wanna know things, why I flagged you over. I listen. But nobody wants to open with me. I guess it's the shit on my body, my messed-up face."

"You don't look like Santy Claus, that's for sure," I laughed. Bravo laughed too and his shiny tooth twinkled like a knife in water.

"My old man beat me, my mother cried, and he beat her. My big brother finally beat him, and I just plain beat it. I found a family in the system, until I did my time and they kicked me out. But I'm finding my way. I watched the birds in the yard, I read the books in the library. From where I stand, I done pretty good."

"And what did the books tell you?"

"I found poetry. It has its own magic, like a lost language. It has its own secrets."

"Which are…?"

"Which is, you'll never understand until you write one yourself."

With that, I got up to move, I still had some ground to cover. Bravo gave me a fist bump, 'k i l l' on his right knuckles, 'l o v e' on the left.

"You heading south, down 119?"

"Always. Heinzeville, about 7 miles out, the great grandfather gave the land for a school. I always drive that way to the coast. It's like I belong to something."

"You'll be passing La Bahia, where they locked up Fannin and his men, before they slaughtered them. Walt Whitman wrote about it in 'Leaves of Grass'. Small world, eh Maddock?"

"Never been smaller. You take it easy, Bravo."

"I got my Savior, Maddock…"

'Hear now the tale of a jetblack sunrise,

*Hear of the murder in cold blood of four hundred and twelve young men.'…*he intoned.

I turned away then. It wasn't far to the car and before long I was gone.

MUSTANG ISLAND

There are two ways onto the island unless you wash ashore or fall out of a plane. I came on from the eastern side, across the ferry to Pt. A and on down the spit of land they call Mustang Island, part of the Padre Island spit that runs clear to Brownsville, 120 miles further south to Mexico. The Mayan King was most of the way west to the Corpus Christi side of Mustang, about 12 miles. Mustang was built up now, unlike in the early days when the denizens were fishermen and shrimpers, rummies, and un-landed gentry. These days the big money had come and the homes were expensive and the *hoi polloi* still mowed the lawns, served the drinks, ran the register. Yet everyone is rich on the ocean, at least while facing out to sea.

The Mayan King was new and the money *nouveau,* drugs and flesh drove the bargain and, well, the story is old as time. It had set up shop down some ways from the Mayan Princess, playing off the delightful hotel that had been a bright spot on the Island for many years. It was a fancy residence now, The Princess, rented to snowbirds, occupied by owners, some part-time, and was the gracious old dowager along this stretch of the coast. It was a reminder of what had been and when I pulled up the circled drive and checked into my room I remembered driving past many years earlier, wondering if I might ever stay there. It featured views of the Gulf and a shuttle every evening to the casino at The Mayan King, kitchens in the rooms, its own beach and several pools. A real delight, but I was a little holed up in my mind. So I pitched everything on the bed and started a smoke on the balcony. I was 3 floors up, but I wasn't a jumper.

Before I called Marie I needed to clear a few things up at the Casino, locate Leah, the little dancer, if I could, make arrangements with Lavon and the Bear. I had it all planned out in my head, but my plans had lately gotten a little loosey-goosey. I didn't want to drop the butter knife on my lap with this crew. Judging by the cats at the Amarillo Boys Club, there was plenty pain on the menu.

So I took my usual shower, did my usual shave, and sat on the bed and lifted the phone. I called the Prairie View motel in Amarillo, to my old buddy Trey who picked up on the first ring.

"You trying to hatch that phone, Trey?"

"Well, well Mr. Maddock. Or rather, Maddock. Things have sure got peaceful since you left. Three days, is it? It's the wonder of wonders."

"How's ole Willoughby makin' out, Trey?"

"He's just fine, sir. They're taking the wire out of his jaw and he's fixin' to eat everything in sight. He's a bachelor, you know, and is getting mighty used to the food in hospital, reading the paper and la de dah. If it wasn't for his jaw being the size of a melon, I'd think he was gold brickin.'"

"Well, that's good. Tell me, is Lavon still around or is he back in New Mex? I need to reach him."

"He moved in with Dolores, sir. They're an item. A hot mess of an item. But I ain't s'posed to mention him at all, sir. Something about cold porridge better served hot. Something like that. Anyway, he skedaddled. Poof"

"You seen Bear?"

"He's around, you just wouldn't know it. He poked his head in last night late, wanting to see if I had heard from you. That's about all."

"Do you know how to reach Lavon?"

"Yes sir."

"Give me the number, ok? And send Willoughby my love."

"Right. You're still the boss, sir. It's 806, blah blah blah blah...." and the phone went 'click', the line went dead. Good ole Trey. He was learning fast.

After that I dialed out to Marie, south Florida, and she answered on the third ring. I was sitting on the side of the bed, but when she answered I had to stand up.

"M & H Investigations," she said.

"Hello H, this is M," I said.

"Oh, Maddock. Where have you been? The pot roast will be burnt." She almost squealed, there was such a delight in her voice.

"Honey, I just made a left turn at the Gulf of Mexico. I'm almost home."

"Please hurry. I don't think I can stand it much longer. You love me don't you. Love love love me?"

"Oh I do. I do…are you good? Have you layed down a tan yet? Do you see me in your dreams, the way I see you?"

"You're the moon and stars. I love you so. I love you so…"

On and on, hearts almost to the bursting, passion and desire, anguish at our brief separation. There had never been a feeling such as this, there would never be a feeling such as this. Pity the world for not being us…

"And how are you M? Did you save the Indian maiden? Did you clean up the town, sheriff?"

"I did all of that and more. And I will tell you. But first, tell me, Marie, have we had any calls for M & H? Does anyone need a gumshoe?"

"One call, a gentleman was seeking our services. He was quite cryptic, as I imagine he would be, needing a Private Investigator. He said he would try back when you were here, wanted to speak only to the principal. I may not have come off quite Nancy Drew enough for him. I told him I expected you within the week and he said he would call back. Not bad for only a few days in business, with no advertisement and no listing as yet. What do you think? I wish I had reeled him in."

"I think…I think we are going to have a change of plans. I want you to understand that sometimes, this time, you may need to trust me, no questions. As I trust you. There are some very difficult people, people I have crossed, maybe…

"Let me begin again. I want you to throw some things together, change of clothes, overnight bag, one bag, as light as you can make it, and quick. There is a place you mentioned where we would have our first morning together…if you remember it, say yes but no names, ok?"

"Yes."

"I will call you in two hours, at that place. If we lose track of each other, you know who to call, right? So that we can link up."

"Yes. Are we in trouble, darling?"

"I shouldn't think so, darling, not at the moment, but we are not taking any chances…I'm through taking chances. When you have your bag together, lock things down, out the back, up the alley. I will fill you in as soon as we are together. Watch your tail…"

"I thought that was your job…"

"You know, I have never met anyone like you before. I was lost and now I'm found. Check your watch…2 hours. Tell them you are Mrs. Smith, expecting a call."

"Hurry, darling."

I hung up.

Then I dropped down to the lobby and joined the crowd milling around, waiting for the shuttle. I had four hundred in my pocket and was gonna put it all on red, rhymes with dead. Or black, throw him in a sack. Made no matter to me. From here all the way to the old man in Chicago, they were all of a piece. Poor dead Charlie meant nothing to them. But he meant plenty to me, and I'm sorry, I was eager to make them pay. So I put on a happy face and climbed on board the van.

The driver said, "Everybody feeling lucky?" And everybody said, "Yeah, yay!" and I smiled too. For no reason did I smile. Or wait, for one reason did I smile. I smiled because they were not done with me yet, this crew. And they were undoubtably closing in. I could feel them closing in, getting closer. And I stared out the van at the ocean, curling into shore, the gulls, the beachcombers, and could just barely make out the muted thunder of the Gulf. Lightning flashed in the distance, on the far horizon.

I was the smiling devil in their dreams now…only they didn't know it. And I saw my face reflected in the glass, and that too made me smile…